HALLUCINOGEN

Kaitlyn Smith

HALLUCINOGEN

Copyright © 2025 Kaitlyn Smith

First printing, 2025

Printed in the United States of America

This is a work of fiction. The story, all names, character, and incidents portrayed in this production are fictitious. No identification with actual persons (living or deceased), places, buildings, and products is intended or should be referred.

Edited by: Anna Keesey of Curly Quotes Editing LLC

Book Cover by: Miblart

ISBN: 979-8-218-66409-1

DEDICATION

For those who wish to lay their heads among the stars.

HALLUCINOGEN

The Tree of Knowledge

Genesis 2:17

My eyes burned, focused solely on the sight in front of me. They begged me to blink, but I refused, preferring to engrave the image in my mind. *Can this be real?*

I feared that if my eyes parted ways, the sight would disappear like a figment of my imagination or a dream I could only half remember. My stomach turned and twisted in turmoil. I wanted to cry, but no tears came. But more than that, I wanted to scream or laugh, yet no sound escaped my lips. I sat stone still, as if the planet before me stared back and if I dared to move it would too.

This was huge. A breakthrough unlike anything we've seen in centuries. This was undeniably something the government wouldn't be able to feign recognition for. We'd be talked about for decades, published in papers, learned about in schools…

Why do I feel so uneasy? The pit of my stomach filled with rocks and dread chilled my blood as fear wound its cold fingers through my mind. *Where did it come—*

"Cap!"

I tore my eyes away from the screen, blinking. Cheering and clapping filled my ears from the mess hall just behind me. The crew was ecstatic.

"Our names are going to be plastered all over the galaxy!" Finnegan held the sides of his head, his glasses tilted on his nose as his curly red hair fell into his eyes.

"We're about to be plastered in a minute!" Jones held a bottle of vodka to her lips, taking a generous gulp before cheering loudly.

Though I understood their excitement, I couldn't help the trembling of my hands or the way my stomach churned as my mind filled with questions. A chill settled over my skin, my hair rising.

"*Come join us*," Hoku signed, a smile on their lips.

I watched the group for a minute, staring at the people around me. Jones was strong and resilient. With each movement of her bronzed arms in the artificial light, her muscles rippled with controlled power. Every fiber of muscle under her skin was a testament to her training and disciplined character. Her voice was loud and gravelly, but low as it resonated through the air in a hum. She kept her hair twisted into eccentric braids that ended at her shoulders, golden pieces adorning each strand that twinkled in the light like her own set of stars.

Hoku, a non-human from a planet long forgotten, watched Jones and Finnegan celebrate. Their face was humanoid in shape, but all similarities stopped there. Twin pairs of crimson eyes gleamed from the low light, each set moving independently, hinting at a heightened awareness humans could only try to fathom. Their lips spread wide, bearing several rows of sharp, onyx-like teeth, tilting their head to the side in their own eerie version of a smile. Fur covered the visible parts of their body, and their legs were digitigrade like that of a panther, with large hands and sharp claws. They towered above the other two, their double-pointed ears nearly touching the ceiling as they moved. Since their vocal cords were unable to reproduce human phonetics, they opted to learn sign language to communicate.

Beside Jones and Hoku, Finnegan perched on the table, seemingly almost out of place among the giants before him. His red curls gleamed, springing in every direction like a halo of copper wire. Thin black glasses sat, slightly crooked, upon his nose. His frame was delicate, the outline of his collarbone and shoulders showing through his jumpsuit which seemed two sizes too large. Despite his nervous look and the anxious tapping of his hands, there was a sharpness in his gaze. He wore a broad smile as he talked with the others.

"Y'all go ahead." I waved a hand of dismissal. "Enjoy yourselves." I turned back to the screen, ignoring their whines and pleas. I sighed, concern still gripping me by the throat. I pulled up the coordinates, double checking we had them right. We've been here before, but . . .

I looked out the window to stare at the planet suspended in the void of space, the soft glow of its sun creating a hazy light around its edges. It loomed, boundless and commanding, dwarfing Earth's familiar contours. The planet seemed closer in scale to Neptune, yet it was infinitely more enchanting. Its surface shimmered with deep crimson and regal purple carved into its landmasses and set against oceans of profound royal blue. Above, clouds hung in an ethereal dance, soft pinks and whites intertwining in a slow, hypnotic waltz. Two moons drifted in steady orbit at opposite ends of the horizon. One blazed fiery orange, illuminated by its own glow. The other was a gentle, verdant green. Together they framed the planet as if guarding its tranquil journey through space.

For a moment, the fear that gripped my nerves so tightly began to loosen. This planet wasn't just habitable. It felt…perfect. A golden promise in the cold expanse of space. A true Goldilocks world balanced and waiting. It wasn't far from Earth, poised just beyond the outskirts of the last warping zones. So why hasn't it been found yet?

"Chug! Chug! Chug!"

I turned back to the mess behind me. Cups were already strewn around the bridge, the vodka bottle already empty. Hoku was knelt under Jones as she poured a fresh bottle of tequila down their throat. They all grinned, cheers from Finnegan ringing through the air.

I shook my head, a small smile tugging at the corners of my mouth. Maybe it's not so bad. I rolled my neck, feeling the stress and tension that had built up in my shoulders begin to release. Maybe it's a good thing. I took a deep breath, feeling my lungs expand, focusing on the way my muscles felt as my diaphragm stretched before I blew out the air. My eyes trailed over the planet once more before I stood.

Making my way over to the small party, I saw Finnegan stumble and spill the drink in his hand as he laughed. The liquid fell against the ground, the fake gravity of the ship pulling it into an oval and away from its center, creating long tendrils reaching for some sort of end.

"Whoa, whoa, party foul," I said. They stopped to look at me as if holding their breath. "I think that means you need to chug the rest of your drink to make up for it." I looked at Jones as she smiled, her eyes gleaming in the ship's light. Hoku clapped excitedly.

"Yeah, Fin!" Jones slapped him on the shoulder, further sloshing his drink out of the cup as the sound echoed through the room.

Finnegan smiled before putting the cup to his lips and downing the contents.

"Let's get the party started then, huh?" I reached for a cup as they smiled and cheered at my words.

Flesh of Gods, Bone of Men

Genesis 2:23 & Psalm 82:6

The walls blurred together as I stumbled down the corridor. The alcohol had stalled my nervous system and numbed my body, so I trailed my right hand along the cool metal of the ship, letting my fingernails catch and pull at the indentions where screws sat. The walls groaned as the metal contracted in the cold void of space. There were no windows on the ship, save for the front. Dim florescent light filled the halls, dust floating freely in the fake gravity. *How did we even get here?*

My eyes tilted back into my head as memories resurfaced.

This is my home. At least for the last eight years it has been. Before that, I only knew of a cold, dark cell. A heavy sigh pushed from my lungs. I'd spent nearly a decade in that ugly concrete box only to revel in a metal one now. We had fake freedom upon this ship dubbed *Revelations*. I laughed at the name. *How ironic.*

My feet caught on a supply box on the floor and the world swayed as I spun, catching myself with both hands outstretched to the walls. I breathed for a moment, facing the way I had just come. I tilted my head to the left slowly, watching the world undulate before closing my eyes.

It seemed like so long ago, the path upon which my life had taken. I recalled the day they opened my cell door. None of us on this ship could ever go back. This ship was our world, our home. There were no open arms to receive us back there. But, with this new discovery, maybe that could be renegotiated. Both fortunately and unfortunately, we're no ordinary ship with an ordinary crew, as cliché as it sounds.

The government began a special division about fifty years ago. They called it *Revanche*. We were to recover, research, and resupply. Our missions were exhausting and difficult, often called a course of death by other supply ships. Everyone knew what you were, and everyone knew what you were meant to do. Other supply ships stayed out of our way, and communication stations only provided us with green lights to move in for refueling.

Save for the few orders we received, we were completely isolated, tasked with mining ice and ore from meteors, landing on moons and other planets to collect samples, and retrieve any old scrap or metal that surrounded the Earth. Anything and everything we found must be analyzed, the data packaged into a small pod and sent back to Earth. The walls of the lab were covered in hundreds of tiny vials of dirt, sand, and rocks of every texture and color imaginable.

Finnegan's notebook was littered with scribbles of unbelievable landscapes, and small picture disks were stacked at the corner of the main desk with biometrics and data samples written in Jones's handwriting. Papers honeycombed with patterns of different elements and red lines and circles denoting different parts of sediment layers covered every nook and cranny of the lab. Some of the papers were singed at the edges from burn tests that got out of hand. All our work and data were to be signed at the bottom by different names from Earth, none of it allowed to be claimed as our own.

The collection and analysis itself weren't necessarily hard. That was routine by now. The real challenge was landing and taking off in a ship that was designed with aerodynamics as an afterthought.

The ship was a bulky, lumbering beast at best, seeming to actively resist the idea of flight. Every descent it preferred to perform a chaotic dance of twists and jolts before coming to a halt by shallowly burying its belly in the ground. Granted, it was more or less what the ship was meant to do. With more than seventy percent of the ship dedicated to storing cargo and fuel, the bottom was built like a tank. It would take a lot of force to make even so much as a dent in it. That being said, it wasn't a luxurious metal box, by any means, but it got the job done. *Mostly.*

Maintenance was a never-ending chore on *Revelations.* Each morning, we wake up to a new alert from the bridge. Whether it be a hydraulic leak, a fried circuit, or a coolant issue, it didn't matter. Each alert came with a frantic scramble to patch it and cross our fingers that we reached our next destination. The ship barely held itself together, more miracle than a machine. Jones was convinced it barely met the standards set for government ships, much less one with a research team.

And yet, *Revelations*, in all its junk-worthy glory, wasn't just limping its way through space. It was warping to unknown locations. That was the worst part—how terrifyingly unpredictable the old tech was. Revanche would send us coordinates with next to no information, leaving us to figure it out, but our clunker of a ship would only get us so close.

More than once, we'd emerged from a warp into a meteor belt or on the outskirts of some planet's gravitational pull, our own ship's system working against us. We'd barely survived those, barely repaired the ship and barely taken a breath, before we were given new tasks, new coordinates, and new work. After so many close calls, we'd gotten wiser. Or at least warier.

Now when given new coordinates, we'd warp just shy of whatever uncharted hellscape Revanche sent us to. Most of the time it worked, if only buying us peace of mind. But sometimes it felt as if the universe itself was testing how far it could push us before we gave out.

I opened my eyes as the dizziness receded, the smooth gray of the walls greeting me once more. My gaze wandered to the chipped and flaking red paint of the ceiling. Symbols that eluded me covered every inch of the dark gray metal. A chaotic masterpiece, each symbol moved from thick to thin strokes of paint, twisting and curling into serrated edges. Each character spiraled outward into another, running together like crimson vines in dizzying patterns latticing the hall. The fluidity of each line was graceful and smooth, the dim light making it seem they were etched into the ship itself. *Hoku's work.*

When they first arrived on the ship, they asked to write blessings upon the walls for safety. Each of the words strewn about the ceilings of our ship was a message, a promise of safe passage, or perhaps a plea. I was never the type to believe in superstitions, but somehow, either by co-incidence or sheer luck, we had managed to be the longest surviving *Revelations* crew to date.

I pursed my lips. At eight years strong, it was almost impossible to believe that the other crews who bore our name had only survived a few months to years at best. We were well known by other supply ships, and we often caught them eyeing us when we passed, as if they couldn't believe we were still alive either. A ghost ship steering toward death but unwilling to die.

I turned, letting my hands fall from the walls as I con-tinued toward my chamber.

I was the first recruit. From what I was told, Revanche combs through the files of inmates in prisons around the Earth, searching for, well, I don't know. Out of the countless prisoners sentenced to death, a select few are offered a chance to trade their cold cells for the stars. Signing your name at the bottom of that paper meant you were giving everything to this ship and accepting the burdens associ-ated, be it the ugly black jumpsuits or the promise of a brutally short life. It didn't matter.

Officially, the project was pitched as a solution to over-crowded death row prisons, a way to thin the ranks of those waiting for the executioner. Unofficially, it was rumored to offer inmates a slim chance at redemption. People whispered that with a big enough discovery it was possible to return to some semblance of a normal life. So, when the opportunity was offered, I didn't hesitate to sign. Death held no meaning to me, but at least this way I felt a false sense of freedom. If they wanted a captain for this ship, then so be it. I would force myself to fit the mold so long as I didn't have to go back.

Jones joined me aboard next. A former war general, she had earned her infamy on the frontlines of a rebellion. Her tactics were ruthless and cruel, but she was unshakable. She had nearly single-handedly dismantled the official governing body of her home country, leaving behind a confirmed two hundred kills which included seventeen high profile political figures. She was powerful in her own right but, her weakness lay in her son. She turned herself in for him, surviving months of disgusting torture and without her as their leader, the rebellion crumbled. But Jones wasn't just a soldier. Beneath her hardened exterior was a mind finely tuned to machines and science. She had an uncanny ability to dissect and rebuild anything mechanical. Her mind had kept her army in the fight. Anything she got her hands on, she could rebuild out of old junk for her own people. If anyone could keep *Revelations* afloat, it was her. Our chief engineer knew the ship like the back of her hand, inside and out.

Finnegan and Hoku came together, like a package deal. From what they've shared, they were imprisoned in the same facility, separated by only a few feet and reinforced steel bars. During brief lulls in guard shifts, Finnegan taught Hoku sign language, their silent exchanges bridging the gap of vastly different worlds.

Hoku is the heavy lifter, their non-Earthling physiology making them a marvel of agility and strength. Watching them move through space was as unsettling as it was inspiring, a blend of strength and dexterity that was hauntingly inhuman. Before boarding our ship, Hoku was notorious for raiding supply ships at the edge of the galaxy, leaving a trail of destruction and death in their wake. A total of forty-seven ships, looted and slaughtered, stained their hands. Despite Earth's best interrogation tactics, Hoku refused to reveal their home planet, choosing to be executed and dissected in a lab over cooperation.

Finnegan's crimes were cut from a different cloth but no less destructive. A world-renowned hacker, he made a name for himself selling political secrets and sowing chaos for the highest bidder. His rap sheet included election interference, stock market crashes, citywide outages, and broadcast sabotage. The list went on. He treated global systems like his personal playground. His downfall only came when he leaked the preferences of a prominent businessman, leading to a scandal so severe it ended in suicide. Some secrets, it seems, couldn't be hushed with money, and Finnegan found himself behind bars, awaiting his dance with death. Now Finnegan serves as our tech analyst.

The beginning of our journey as a crew was bitter and riddled with disloyalty. Arguments ensued like alarms on the ship, constant bickering and finger-pointing rotting away our ability to work together. It didn't seem like we'd ever get along. There were many times when petty disagreements came to blows, leaving us bloodied and broken. We were a group of individuals so hellbent on self-preservation we were willing to kill those we shared space with. It was clear we were terrified. Too damaged to let others in and too prideful to admit it. We had barely survived those barbaric months.

Eventually, we learned struggling didn't have to be done alone and neither did surviving. We left the past behind, choosing to watch Earth from above, a place we no longer belonged. Those first few months, we'd sit just outside Earth's orbit, staring down at the familiar greens and blues of a world that exiled us.

White, fluffy clouds hung in the atmosphere surrounded by a cacophony of land and sea and lit with the powerful glow of the sun. We were left to wonder if we'd ever set foot there again, knowing we couldn't.

So why don't we run? I let out a dry chuckle as I stumbled down the hall. Who wouldn't try to escape? A ragtag crew of criminals handed a second chance on a silver platter. Some people in those cells could only dream of boarding a warp ship stocked with supplies. It's almost too good an opportunity to pass up. But it never works. The last few who tried got turned into grim examples of Revanche's control. They gave us a barely functioning rust bucket for a reason.

Unlike their nuclear-powered beauties, we burn through fuel like kindling. Four warps and we're dead in the void, just sitting ducks with nowhere to go.

I push a hand to the door sensor of my room, and it opens with a gush of air. The walls are bare. A single pillow and beige blanket lie haphazardly across a thin mattress. I kicked my boots off, sighing as my aching body sinks into the bed.

This was it for us. Not that chunk of dirty rock we used to know. *No,* this *is home.*

Dust and Ashes

Job 30:19

My eyes snapped open. Flashing lights sliced through the darkness of the room in a strobing red. The piercing wail of the siren filled my ears, drowning out my frantic breaths as adrenaline surged through my veins. My lungs heaved with stress as I scrambled to my feet, fumbling to get dressed as the frenzy of alarms started. My body shook, my feet nearly tripping over themselves. The airlock hissed as my door slid open, and Jones rushed past in a blur, her expression sharp with urgency and worry.

"What happened?" I yelled over the blaring alarm.

She turned to me, her curls loose from her braids and tousled around her face, her pupils like pinpoints. "I don't know!" She yelled back.

These aren't the usual alarms. No this felt worse. The shrill wails pierced my ears. Panic rooted in my gut, spreading to my throat where it lay as a lump. A hiss, barely audible, sounded to my right. Finnegan, disoriented, stepped out of his chamber. Hoku peeked their head over him, grimacing in pain and covering their ears with their hands.

"Come on!" I motioned at the two to follow me.

Making our way from the chambers to the bridge, it was clear what the issue was: *everything*. The oxygen was low, water was leaking, the coolant systems were damaged, the engines . . . The ship had somehow sustained a critical hit.

How did we not feel it? The asteroids around us were so far away, could one have really slammed into us while we slept? *Impossible.* An impact of that magnitude, that set off this many alarms, would've jarred us awake.

"Shut those damn alarms off!" My words were laced with anger and confusion. The sounds stopped, silence gripping the room as the red lights continued to flash. Finnegan stared up at me from his panel with wide eyes, awaiting my next order. "What the hell happened?"

Jones scrolled through the list of warnings on the large main screen. They were endless. "Almost all systems are offline, Cap. Everything is just . . . gone." She began scrolling faster, the words flashing by.

My heart raced as the codes and numbers flew along the screen in a nauseating whirlwind. I closed my eyes for a moment, trying to collect my thoughts, dizzy from the situation at hand. *We still have power. We're not completely fucked.*

"Where's the damage centered?" I opened my eyes. All their eyes remained on me. Finnegan bit at his fingernails while Hoku pulled nervously at their ears.

"Most of the warnings are coming from the southern side by the hold–"

"What about our warning systems? Shouldn't they have gone off before impact?" Finnegan cut Jones off, his voice small and scratchy. We stared at him for a moment, trying desperately to come up with answers, but none were forth-coming.

"I mean, it should've," Jones shook her head, her eyes glazing over as she scrunched her brow in thought. "Never mind an impact of this caliber, where our backside is acting like it's been *torn away*, should've sent us flying. Do you think an asteroid could do damage like this?"

Hoku shook their head in response. We stared at the screen, critical alarms filling its entirety and flashing bright red in the eerie silence.

A chill hugged my skin. I blew out a breath as I clasped my hands behind my head. A million thoughts ran through my mind, none of them good.

"What do we do?" Finnegan's voice was barely audible as if he were asking himself more than me. "Are we going to run out of air?"

All eyes were focused on me, awaiting my direction. The glow of the red alarms flickered across their faces, casting sharp, fleeting shadows that stretched and twisted with every flash. The darkness between pulses seemed alive, swallowing each of them before pushing them forward to reveal the harsh, raw edges of panic etched into their eyes. *What do I say?*

"False alarms? Broken sensors? Could be small hole?" Hoku signed quickly, cutting out words as panic flooded their shaking hands.

I felt relieved as the crew's attention turned to them. "You think a couple of wrong way wires could cause every alarm in our system to go haywire?" My voice was steady, but my breath was trembling.

Hoku's eyes wandered along the ceiling and floor as if they were tracing the wires themselves, before meeting mine once more. "*Could be possible. Wires are looped. Signal got stuck. Infinite loop?*" After they finished signing, they shrugged.

Infinite loop? The way Hoku stood, wringing their hands and shifting their weight seemed to lack confidence. *Fuck it.* What other chance did we have?

"Finnegan, see if there are any signals or cameras online that aren't blaring fucking warnings so we can try to assess the damage from here." I put my hands on my hips as he worked.

His fingers moved across the interface with precision. Every tap, every swipe, and every touch was part of an intricate dance of calculations and code, a choreography only he seemed to understand. The lenses of his glasses caught the flickering holographic readouts, shining them back like a screen of their own, communicating. Despite the nervous energy buzzing around him, his gaze was keen.

"I can't find anything on that end with a good enough signal, sir. I'm sorry." Finnegan continued to stare at the screen, desperately searching.

I ground my teeth in frustration.

Jones let out a disappointed sigh. "What do we do?"

Jones's voice echoed in my ears. My eyes met with the planet outside our window, the vibrant purples and blues obnoxiously off-putting now. *No, no, no.* "Good news. We have an old ship that runs on fuel, therefore there's no reactor meltdown to worry about." Their faces remained stoic. "Bad news. We're running out of air, water, and fuel. We need to assess the damage and fast. So, let's get to it."

With a clap of my hands their backs straightened, determination smoothing the worried wrinkles on their foreheads. *Yeah, we can do this. It's nothing new.*

I ran my hands down my face as I stared at the large screen once more before turning away and starting toward the cargo bay that comprised the southern end of the ship. The crew followed close behind.

The flashing red light was endless, throwing the ship into inky darkness before drowning it in an unbearably urgent red. The ship remained excruciatingly quiet, as if it were holding its breath. The only noise was our footsteps echoing against the hard metal walls of the ship, filling the silence with an inconsistent beat while my mind wandered about what may lie beyond.

No one spoke, preferring silent company over half-baked thoughts and empty promises. We knew anything that escaped our lips now was hopeless speculation or a lucky assumption.

Even in the suffocating darkness, the ship's familiar layout guided us forward. We moved past the mess hall, the lab, the stacked supply shelves, and the quiet stillness of our personal quarters. The cargo bay was just ahead. But as we passed the final hall, our steps faltered, and we came to an abrupt halt. Looming before us, the heavy emergency doors stood sealed tight, their reinforced panels glinting dully in the red flickering light. My heart sank.

"That's not a good sign," Jones muttered.

I turned to face them, anxiety pushing its long fingers down my throat, my stomach searing and churning. I could feel the blood leave my face, my cheeks tingling as sweat beaded along the small of my back and brow. My body was on high alert, irrational thoughts swarming my mind, my muscles tense and breathing shallow. It felt as if we were sitting ducks, prey stuck in a trap while our demise sat just outside, waiting.

Focus. What's the immediate danger? Oxygen. If we lose our oxygen, we die.

"Finnegan, pull up the oxygen sensors. How much do we have remaining?"

He pulled out his holo, a small handheld interface that resembled its counterpart, his console on the bridge. "About sixty-two percent, sir." As the flashing lights dimmed, his face was illuminated by the blue glow of the holo gripped tightly in his hands.

Sixty-two? That could be worse. "Okay, first things first, we find that leak and we patch it. That means we need someone to assess the damage, and since we can't access that half of the ship, we need to head to the dock." I turned on my heel before they had a chance to protest.

The trek to the dock was just as silent and tepid as our first walk. The echoing of footsteps behind me was the only consolation that I wasn't in this alone.

As I stole a glance upward, a cold wave of dread washed over me. The once familiar and ever present flaky crimson symbols were gone, the red of the emergency lights melting them into itself to reveal illusory empty panels above. A suffocating sense of fear struck me. Hoku's blessings, the words they had so painstakingly scattered among the ceiling of our ship seemed to vanish. Our fragile tether of protection snapped, leaving only an unsettling void of red in its place. It seemed as if it were a warning, like the harbinger of death was lying in wait for us.

"Captain?"

Finnegan. I hadn't even realized I'd stopped walking.

"You all right?" Finnegan asked, looking at me quizzically.

The rest of the crew watched me with worried eyes.

I nodded. His eyes softened with concern, looking up as the darkness surrounded us but his eyes were back on me when the red flash of light returned. "Let's keep moving." I motioned for them to continue following my lead.

As we delved deeper into the ship, the damage was unrelenting. The walls became jagged as pipes had ruptured through the walls, cutting wires and stripping bolts, just to dump their contents on the floor. Sparking wires dangled overhead from bent and broken metal panels, creating small flickers of light. The smell of chemicals and water permeated the air.

Once at our destination, I tried the sensor for the door, but it refused to budge. It stood staring at us in the gloom and shimmering sparks. I pushed at it with my shoulder, begging the airlock to release. As I pushed, my right foot slipped, my body pitching to the side. I barely caught myself on the doorframe.

"Hoku, give me a hand."

They pushed a shoulder against the door as well but to no avail.

"Here, let me help." Jones assumed the same position, all three of us willing the door to open, but it remained stubborn.

Finnegan stayed back, head tilted, observing. When the door refused to move with the three of us pushing against it, Hoku tried prying at the door with a piece of metal as Jones and I pushed, hoping leverage would help. A sharp hiss sliced through the air as gas released from the pressurized lock. For a moment, the door held steadfast, tension pulling at our muscles. Then, with a shuddering jolt, the door wrenched open as a rush of air escaped the lock. We took a moment to breathe, staring into the room before us.

I put a hand over my mouth, tugging downward. The uncanny feeling of danger that seemed to have gone dormant returned. *What am I doing?*

Eight suits hung in perfect alignment along the wall, their dark fabric reflecting a metallic sheen in the low light. Scratches—wear and tear from countless missions—decorated the plating, and faint discolorations from exposure to alien atmospheres and various abrasions adorned the suit's respective helmets. The visors, dark and indecipherable, flashed in quiet harmony with the emergency lights.

"You all stay put." I didn't even bother looking at them as I moved to grab my suit from the wall.

"You've got to be kidding me." Jones moved forward, bewildered.

Hoku waved their hands frantically in concern.

"It's nowhere near safe out there. I don't have any cameras or sensors to tell you where the asteroids are or if one decides to head your way," Finnegan whined.

I waved a hand, dismissing their concerns.

"*You go, I go*," Hoku signed before moving to grab their suit from the wall too. They stared at me in surprise when I grabbed their wrist.

"Absolutely not." I pushed their hand away. "I'll be fine. I don't want any of you tagging along in case things get shifty out there. Besides, I'm just going to take a peek." A faint, but fake, smile of reassurance graced my lips, but it wasn't convincing, even to me.

Jones shook her head. "You're insane. Safety protocol says at least two crew members are to go outside the ship to ensure mitigation of any risks associated with—"

"Being in space. Yes, I know." I pulled up the zipper on the suit, holding the helmet in my hands. "We've made it this far because we have those rules. I understand. But we've also taken risks to survive, and right now is one of those risks. I need each of you alert and, more importantly, alive. I'll be quick, but in the unlikely event that something does happen, I'd rather lose one than two in a situation like this." I locked the helmet into place, communications coming online with an electrified static hum.

"*Don't die.*" Hoku forced a smile through concerned features.

I nodded. "Comms check," I said, turning to Finnegan.

He pulled his holo back out, nimble fingers pressing a few different buttons, finding a channel to connect our signal. A beep resounded and a small light turned on inside the bottom right of the helmet.

"Can you hear me?" Finnegan's voice filtered through the suit filled with static, almost robotic. Not a great signal, but it would do for now. *Make it quick.*

"I can." He nodded at my response. "I'll let you guys know what I find."

With that, I opened the first door into the airlock, clipping myself into the rung near the door to create a safety line to hold on to. A few quick tugs of the rope connecting me to the ship ensured my line was adequate. Air hissed as the chamber depressurized, releasing gas through the different valves.

Moving to face the outer door, silence greeted my ears, the flashing of red from the alarms no longer haunting me. Instead, the door opened, slow and controlled, the lock releasing in two parts. The draining of the airlock clawed at me with a tender force, pulling me away from the ship and into the void.

Space is beyond imaginable. We see it depicted on Earth as this boundless pit, but nothing compared to reality. Even now, as I floated along the outside of the ship, it felt unreal. My breath had all but left my lungs, my mind silenced by the sheer overwhelming beauty it presented.

Space expanded far beyond my fingertips, yet somehow it seemed like I could reach out and pluck a star from the inky void. The light of each star burned in a brilliant fire, swirling within itself as if it were alive. Away from the shield of Earth's atmosphere, light pierced with blinding clarity, unobstructed. Behind the tint of my visor, I had to squint as my eyes adjusted. The silence enveloped me, deafening, sending chills coursing down my spine. Peeling my eyes away, I began to grab the small handholds on the outside of the ship.

As I made my way along the body of the ship, static crackled within my suit. Our signal was weaker, but I didn't stop. I continued to pull myself through the weightless field. As I neared the area of concern, small pieces of debris floated lazily, glinting faintly in the starlight. My hands moved faster, skipping handholds in my hurry. Upon reaching my destination my blood surely left my body.

"Impossible."

Shattered remnants of our ship drifted aimlessly, jagged edges shimmering in the silence of space. Panels, tubing, and fragments of the hull floated, spinning in slow, eerie rotations. Pieces of shattered glass reflected the distant stars, scattering pinpricks of light across the void. The debris expanded in all directions, a mass graveyard of steel and circuitry. A small glob of water moved by me, no friction or gravity to stop its procession as it turned within itself.

We're doomed. The entirety of the southern hull was gone, ripped from the ship and scattered among the stars. I blinked, both in shock and awe, tears pricking at the back of my eyes. *How? How could this happen?*

This was no asteroid. I knew the scars they left behind. An asteroid may scrape along the plating, cause a few dents or rupture a compartment, *but this?* This was complete obliteration. This kind of damage should have sent us spinning, not sitting eerily still in a frictionless expanse. Something was wrong. Something was horribly wrong.

"C-c-cap?" Finnegan's staticky voice echoed through the helmet.

Panic settled in my bones. *What do I say?* They would lose their minds.

"You th-there . . . s-see any-hing?"

I tried to still my trembling body, my mind grasping at anything to explain what could have happened. My eyes drifted to the thrusters, falling upon one of the three fuel shells perfectly intact. Both thrusters had sustained serious damage.

"Nothing we can't handle." The lie was sour on my tongue, and I didn't wait for them to respond. As I turned, my hands faltered, and I froze.

There it was, hanging in the emptiness. Its swirling purples and deep blues gleamed mockingly, vivid and alive against the void with the haloed glow of the orange sun behind it. It felt as if it were watching me, waiting. A cold unease crept along my spine, the ripples of its clouds whispering something I couldn't understand.

As I made my way back to the ship, I refused to move my eyes away from the planet, fearing I would be torn away from the ship if I did.

The Descent

John 3:13

Returning to the dock brought chaos. Their voices overlapped in a cacophony of panic, hungry for answers. The air hummed with fear, and it clung to me like a suffocating fog. I tried to remain stoic as I put away the suit, my knuckles white, mouth dry. As their captain, I should have the answers, but after what I saw I had nothing but questions. The weight of the situation pushed down on me, and for a moment, all I could hear was the pounding of my heart in my ears. Nervous perspiration began to build along my lower back.

"We need to get back to the bridge." Try as I might, my voice still shook.

"Cap—"

"Now." I regarded them with a sense of urgency they all understood.

It took everything in my body not to sprint back to the bridge, my muscles tense. We followed our previous path, the red flashing lights a warning now more than ever, synchronized with the pounding in my ears, showing us the ship's quick, shallow heartbeat.

Once at the bridge I began to pace, desperately thinking of our next move.

"Tell me something good." I waved a hand at the crew.

Each of them scrambled for their holos, searching for any sign of luck. If nothing else, I wanted false hope, some sense of security even if it was worthless.

Jones looked up. "We still have full power in two parts of the ship, but only partial in most others."

"We're at fifty-eight percent oxygen, so we're not losing it as fast as we thought." Finnegan adjusted his glasses.

"*Leak could be small,*" Hoku signed. The three of them nodded in unison.

"Good." As I looked past them, my eyes found the planet. Like a lone wolf hunting among the expanse of space, it had found its prey. My jaw clenched as I stared, watching the contours of it, waiting for any slight change, but none came. *It's just a planet.* We'd seen dozens of them. I pinched the bridge of my nose. "How is communication? Can we send a distress signal out? Are there any ships nearby we can intercept?"

"There won't be another ship near us for almost a month. We're on the outskirts." Jones sat at her console with a huff.

Finnegan continued tapping away at his keyboard. "I can't get any signal out farther than half a mile from our ship."

"If we have no point of contact and we won't survive the month it'll take for the next ship to reach us then what do we do?" Jones asked.

Anxiety wound its trembling fingers around my heart. *They're depending on you. Think.* But my mind continued to draw blanks, questions slipping through my grasp and panic surging in my blood.

"*Patch the hole?*" Hoku worriedly signed.

I shook my head. There was no patching that. Even if we managed to seal the oxygen to just the bridge of the ship, we would run out of water. We'd only survive a few weeks at most. My eyes trailed once more to the planet in front of us.

"It's a Goldilocks, right?" I asked. They all nodded as they turned their attention to the planet outside. "Prepare to land."

Their eyes snapped back to me, bewildered.

"Are you serious?" Jones questioned. "Cap, we aren't authorized to land down there, and there's no way our ship could handle it. We haven't even told Revanche—"

"I said prepare to land, and that's an order. The ship is going to have to hold together. Hoku, I want you to start sealing all emergency doors. Seal off the oxygen to the working area of the ship, and grab each of us a suit. Jones, start booting up the engine. We have a third of the working capacity, but it should be enough. And Finnegan, start figuring out a way to boost our signal once we get down there." I leaned both hands on the console in front of me, eyeing the planet, its small sun burning behind it.

"This is insane," Jones muttered as she began preparations.

"I'd rather we take our chances down there than waste away up here. At least on the surface, we have a shot at finding food, water, and there's oxygen."

More alerts began to pop up along the screens as the thrusters came online.

"We only have functionality from thruster two. Fuel cell three is being diverted, but it's only at half capacity." Jones's voice was steady as she worked.

"We'll use the planet's gravitational pull to our advantage," I responded.

"I think I can do it." Finnegan wiped his brow with his hand. "Our small comms still work, and we have the transmitter, so while we're down there I could probably extend an antenna with whatever scraps are left and boost the signal using the atmosphere. It won't go far but it would be farther than what we have now. Possibly to an outer station."

Jones spoke through clenched teeth, her voice teaming with irritation. "There's no guarantee we'd have power or that comms won't be destroyed during landing."

"We will. Don't give up on this old piece of junk yet. She's made a dozen rough landings, and she can handle one more." I patted the console with a reassuring hand as Jones scoffed.

"Preparations are complete," Jones said.

I nodded. "We're go for land. Everyone buckle up." I clapped my hands together, the sound sharp and hollow against the palpable tension.

We donned our suits and buckled in, taking one last breath.

Our ship began its slow limp toward the planet's orbit, thrusters sputtering just enough to push us forward. As we grew closer, it surrendered to the planet's gravitational pull.

We were taking a gamble. There was no way for us to tell how the planet's gravity would affect the ship. If it was too strong, we'd be crushed. Too weak and we might never make it, stuck forever in a downward spiral.

Sweat slicked my forehead as the pressure on my shoulders began to build.

The moment we breached the atmosphere, the ship began to rattle violently. Alarms blared, no longer willing to be silenced, their shrill wails cutting through the roar of entry.

Gravity's unstoppable hand ushered us to the ground, merciless. The metal of the ship glowed white-hot as heat encircled it. I grit my teeth. Clouds whipped around us, the sound unbearable as our ship began to turn and twist. Then the clouds broke, revealing an endless expanse of water below. Panic surged through my body.

"Pull up!" I screamed as the watery grave drew too close.

Jones strained against the weight of the ship, pulling with everything she had.

But we continued to press downward, falling at an immense speed, refusing to budge. Suddenly, our view changed, tilting ever so slightly as the ship's nose turned upward.

Then we hit.

The impact was violent, a bone-jarring collision that sent the ship lurching uncontrollably. Metal screamed as it sheared apart, and sparks began igniting wild flames as the ship careened on its side. The ship groaned under the strain, spinning as chunks of debris tore free and vanished. Glass shattered in explosive bursts, the forestry outside blurring into a chaotic swirl of purple and red as branches tore into the metal panels. Finally, the ship slammed to a halt, its broken frame settling with a tortured creak as it came to rest.

Silence. The alarms had long since gone offline, the ship taking too much damage to try and cry anymore. I let out the breath I'd been holding, my lungs and muscles burning from the effort. I scanned the ship quickly, barely taking in the extent of the damage. *Shit.* There was no way this old girl would fly again.

I closed my eyes, leaning my head back against the headrest as I stared out the broken bridge window. My mind swirled with nothing and everything at the same time. My eyes drifted over the crew as they began to unbuckle, all their suits still intact. *Good, we survived step one. The rest is easy.*

After unbuckling myself, I worked my way through the wreckage.

Finnegan's chest rose and fell quickly, slight tremors holding his hands. Hoku stood calmly to the side, their pinky entwined on the loop near Finnegan's shoulder. Jones hadn't moved. She sat perfectly still, her eyes hazy.

"Everyone okay?"

The only one to respond was Hoku, who nodded their head, a nervous smile twitching at the corners of their mouth.

"All right. Let's get to work. We need to establish a few things first, like figuring out if comms will work and finding food. We still have power though I'm not sure for how long, so we need to work fast."

There was a whisper from Jones. I looked at Hoku who shrugged.

"It says the air is breathable." Her voice was still small, much different to her usual commanding tone. Jones's eyes were focused on the holo in front of her, reading whatever data her suit could garner.

"Yes, it might be, but—"

"The planet is like Earth, right?" Finnegan began to search through his own holo, Hoku moving to peak over his shoulder.

Jones's eyes drifted slowly toward us, glazed over in thought. "It's nearly identical in atmospheric composition. The only difference is the concentration. Oxygen is at 34.7%, carbon dioxide at 0.034%, nitrogen 64.5%, and the pressure outside is 1.38 bar."

"Doesn't excess oxygen cause lung damage? It's poisonous, right? What about the pressure. Won't that hurt us?" My eyes darted to Hoku who stood perfectly fine and to my own feet which were planted firmly on the ground.

"With how many planets we've traveled to, I think we're fine," Jones retorted.

"Usually have failsafe. Or help."

Hoku was right. Before landing on alien planets, we've always monitored the atmosphere and gravitational pull, altering our suits to handle the unfamiliar environments with weights or exoskeletons. As of now, we were without. Luckily, it didn't seem to matter.

Jones continued. "The human body is more adaptable than you think. We're pretty good at handling pressure changes. Besides, it looks like the pressure of the atmosphere and gravitational pull balance out. It might feel a bit heavier to walk, but we should be okay. The oxygen might be a bit of a problem with that fire outside. Our metabolic rates would also increase, meaning our cells would start working and dying a lot faster." She shrugged. "I don't see a problem. The rebreathers in our helmets should filter out any of the nonsense if we ran out of oxygen in the suits."

I shook my head. "We don't know what's in the air. There could be any number of bacteria or other unknowns floating around, so don't get comfortable with that idea."

There are rules to space. Most people don't care to know them and care even less to follow them. When outside the ship in space, you remain as close as possible so you don't float away. Oxygen tanks are checked before and replenished after every mission. If you land on a foreign planet, you *never* remove your suit. You stay on the ship and send out a signal. If you must leave the ship because it was compromised, you stay vigilant and leave in pairs. The atmosphere here isn't an issue, but the things you can't see are. Otherworldly bacteria your body has no clue how to fight, viruses that can infect the bloodstream . . .

Death is always watching on every new planet. But we managed to survive this long, and we could survive this too if we followed the rules.

"Holy . . ." Jones whispered.

My attention snapped to her. Her hand rested on the broken windshield of our ship, the glass crushed beneath her boots as she hoisted herself out using the cabinets as a makeshift foothold.

We moved closer to her, each of our eyes taking in the surroundings as we climbed out of the ship, using the crumpled nose as a ladder to reach the ground. My eyes widened. *It's beautiful.*

The planet was just as mesmerizing down here as it was from orbit. The towering trees stretched skyward, dwarfing Earth's tallest, their immense trunks fading in the hazy distance. I tilted my head back, trying to get a glimpse of the tops, but the sheer scale made me dizzy. The bark of each tree intertwined like large, thick cables, their longs roots dipping in and out of the ground. My breath caught at the colors. *Oh god, the color.*

Deep, rich purples veined with vibrant streaks of crimson painted the trunks and leaves like living rivers. The grass, tall and thin, shimmered with freckles of purple, brushing against our hips and shoulders as it swayed gently. Ashes fell from the sky like fresh snowfall, their gray color making them feel out of place in the obnoxiously vibrant landscape.

Thin trails of fire slithered through the wreckage, hungrily licking at the grass and twisted remains of trees. Our ship lay in ruins, torn apart as if mauled by something monstrous. Entire chunks of the ship were missing, torn away to reveal jagged edges of metal curling inward like broken ribs. The once half-proud vessel had finally caved under its own weight, its belly buried in the earth as if crawling into its own shallow grave, begging for rest. I had never seen it in such disarray. My hands trembled and my heart wrenched. Our ship. *Our home*.

Overwhelmed, I began to back away, wanting to return to the safety of the ship's broken corpse.

"Hey guys, I found something." Finnegan's voice echoed through our suits.

Hoku motioned for us to move closer to the trees.

"*Watch*," they signed.

As Finnegan moved a single gloved hand over the bark of the tree, the colors shifted. The purple moved like a wave, pulsing outward from the touch as if it were made of water and Finnegan's finger the droplet. As the wave expanded beyond the trunk, it was caught among the others surrounding it, flooding each of the surrounding trees with a shimmering wave of scarlet infused purple. I lost my breath once more, the wave dissipating as it retreated into the distance.

"*Like a signal*." Hoku signed as Finnegan began to remove a piece of the bark with his utility knife, another wave of purple crashing through the trees.

My mind faltered, my feet unconsciously moving back. My body screamed with everything it had, warning me, ushering me to hide. It was a feeling I had never felt before, something so wrong it sat in the marrow of my bones. *I've led them to their deaths.*

"Cap?" Jones reached out with a steady hand, an anchor.

My breathing was shallow, my throat dry. As I faced the ship, I stood still, its broken and damaged body pleading with me. *Why is it quiet?* I turned slowly, scanning the sprawling landscape. There wasn't a single noise. No rustling of branches, no whisper of wind through the trees, no calls of unseen creatures, not a single buzz, chirp, or shuffle. *Nothing.*

My eyes drifted to the swaying grass, observing as their tall stalks bent with ease, moving without the faintest sound. It was bizarrely quiet, the stillness of it loud in my ears. Reaching out, I plucked a blade of grass. Thick and viscous pink sap oozed from the wounded stem, but as I held it in the air, the grass didn't dare to move.

My breath hitched as I focused past the grass in my hand to settle on the clouds. They hung in the air, motionless, suspended as if artificial. A faint, sickly, pink hue tinged their otherwise pale forms as they loomed in the distance. My stomach sank, dread clawing through me. Something was disgustingly wrong. My gaze darted back to the ground, vomit collecting in my throat. The grass had stopped moving. Not a single blade crossed or touched. My pulse thundered in my ears.

"Get back to the ship." I moved quickly, dropping the piece of grass to the ground, my legs delighted to get back to safety.

"But we just—"
"Now!"

And The Heavens Were Silent

Revelation 8:1

We sat together in what was left of the bridge, my mind spinning from the previous few moments. It replayed over and over: the clouds, the silence, the sudden stillness of the grass.

"We can't leave the immediate area around the ship. We need to remain where we can see each other, since have no idea what's out there." Each of them stared at me in disturbing obedience, awaiting whatever orders I'd delegate to fix our situation. "Right now, our main focus is returning to Revanche. Finnegan, get a point of contact up and running before we lose power. Hoku, I need you to find food and water for us to survive the night. Jones, start collecting samples. Run them if any of the systems are still up. The western airlock is still in decent condition, so I can work on repressurizing it and we can eat in there." I had checked the oxygen levels left in the ship, and they barely sat at twenty-nine percent. We'd only realistically be able to eat and drink twice with that amount of air. *It will have to do.*

"Hey, Cap?" Jones's brown eyes locked on mine, her expression solemn. "What happens if we get back?"

"*When,*" Hoku corrected, patting her shoulder softly.

Finnegan hugged his knees to his chest. "Yeah. A find like this? We could finally go home."

I let out a sigh, staring at the purple expanse beyond our shattered window. It had been so long since we'd lived any semblance of normalcy.

"I don't know." My voice was quiet, barely a mumble.

Finnegan shrunk into his chair, burying his face in his hands.

Dinner was a meager packet of rice and dried meat Hoku managed to scavenge from the scorched remains of our mess hall, but there was no water to wash it down. We had settled into the airlock, relieved to finally be able to take our helmets off, savoring the unobstructed view of one another's faces.

It had taken quite some time for me to figure out how to divert the ship's dwindling oxygen reserves into the airlock's depressurization system, but with a little bit of elbow grease and closing off the right pipes, it worked. Now, fresh oxygen would cycle through the locks and fill the room, purging the alien air. It was a fragile reprieve amidst the larger, awful reality of our situation. We held on to our false sense of security as we ate.

"Hey, Jones." Finnegan ran his hands through his hair, the red strands falling into his eyes over his glasses. "If there's increased oxygen, how come the plants are huge? Don't they need carbon dioxide?"

"Yes and no." Jones set down the empty packet of rice next to her. "Oxygen helps plants within their root systems.

The more dissolved oxygen in the dirt, the better they're able to perform photosynthesis." She twirled her fork in her hands for a second. "Bigger trees means the possibility of a bigger food chain. Which means more carbon dioxide."

Finnegan scanned the walls of the ship as if looking past them to the outside. "How big?"

"Judging from the trees? Pretty fuckin' big," I responded. "All the more reason to stick together."

"There was an experiment done a while ago," Jones said, her brow furrowed. "I think it was Dr. Kei?" She paused, absent in thought.

Hoku tapped on her knee, and her head snapped to look at the door.

"Everything okay?" Finnegan asked tentatively.

"The light." Her eyes remained unmoving, fixated not on the door, but what lay beyond.

"What?" Finnegan questioned.

"It's filtered. When dinosaurs were around, it was the same way. Dr. Kei replicated it." She cleared her throat. "Back when dinosaurs were around, everything was huge. Earth's atmosphere was comprised of massive concentrations of oxygen, and the light was different than it is today. Not only does the ozone protect against UV, so do trees. Their canopy of leaves filters it out into pure light. Dr. Kei did an experiment that replicated those conditions, growing a tomato plant over thirty feet tall that produced some thirteen *thousand* tomatoes."

"Whoa," Finnegan said in awe, "You think the same thing could be happening here?"

"It's possible. Obviously, the food chain and environmental system on this planet could be vastly different and my theory could be way off." She shrugged. "But those trees are huge for a reason."

"We need to head back out there and get to work. I want to get a signal out as soon as possible and get us off this damn planet." I pulled my helmet back on, feeling the familiar click as it sunk into place forming a seal around my neck. "Jones, I want you to check out the lab. Find anything you can and start analyzing everything. Finnegan and Hoku, I need you both to start working on comms and getting an antenna ready. We're going to have a long night."

As the airlock doors released, the broken body of our ship was revealed to us through dim, flickering lights and sparking wires. Thick, metallic smoke rose from burned circuits as the faint acrid bite of leaking coolant creeped past the filters in the suits. The floor beneath my boots was uneven as I walked, a patchwork path of rubble and buckled plating. Each step sounded heavier than the last, as if the ship were bending under the weight of its own despair.

I sighed. This was the final stop of a proud ship that survived what others said it wouldn't. For eight long years she had been limping between the stars and now she lay to rest. I felt a twinge in my heart as I drew my hand along my broken console, feeling the grooves and shards of glass as they fell to the ground.

"Just a little to the left." Finnegan's voice poured over our suit comms. I looked up to see him standing in the grass, directing an unseen Hoku. I made my way out of the ship toward Finnegan. "Almost," he said.

"What's going on?" I caught sight of Hoku on top of the ship, tearing at broken panels.

"We're trying to get to the auxiliary power line. I know we don't really have a whole lot of power, but if we can splice it, we might be able to divert enough power to the transmitter to boost our signal. Surprisingly, it's still in pretty good condition." Finnegan looked back at his holo and traced an orange line on a map of the ship.

"Isn't the ship currently running on auxiliary power? Are you risking cutting power from the ship?" I crossed my arms as I watched Hoku start rummaging through the wires.

"It should have big yellow lines on it," Finnegan called up. Hoku gave a thumbs up in response. "It might, but honestly, it's worth the risk if you ask me. If we can get the transmitter rebooted with a bigger power source, I may not have to boost the signal as much with a relay or giant antenna. Once our signal is functional, I plan to check the frequencies and make sure there's no interference. Then I can try widening the signal." His nose scrunched, and his gaze focused as he watched his friend on top of the ship.

"And if it doesn't work?"

He shook his head at my words. "It has to work, so it will." He continued to stare straight ahead, his eyes only moving to look at his holo before quickly returning to Hoku. "That's the one!" He voiced enthusiastically.

Hoku turned to us, a wide toothy grin spread across their face as they held the large wire in their hands. They stood, tugging at the wire, begging it to loosen away from the others for better access. As they pulled, the panel beneath their foot broke away.

My stomach dropped.

Hoku lost their footing, tumbling from their perch. The jagged maul of the ship rising toward them as they fell, landing with a sickening thud. A sharp crack resounded as their helmet smacked against the ship.

"Shit!"

Both Finnegan and I ran toward them as they lay unmoving upon the ground. I rolled them over onto their back. A hairline fracture had split across the visor of their helmet, spidering outward as the fragile glass pushed against the strain. A faint hiss followed as air began to leak. Panic set in as I scrambled to seal the crack, hands trembling.

"The rebreather!" Finnegan shook my shoulder with one hand while his other gripped Hoku's side.

Shit. With only slight hesitation, I removed Hoku's helmet, ripping the rebreather from it and pulling it over their mouth and nose. We waited, desperately hoping their lungs would move, but they remained still.

Finnegan pushed me aside, starting compressions, tears trailing down his face. "Come on, you idiot. Breathe!"

Jones stepped down from the broken bridge window.

"What the hell happened?"

"He slipped from the top." My finger rose, pointing toward the apex of the ship.

The compressions weren't working. Finnegan's hands moved frantically, each press on Hoku's chest growing more and more desperate. Sweat mixed with tears dripped down his face and onto the visor of his helmet.

"Come on, Hoku," he begged through gritted teeth, his voice cracking as hope began to slip away. Hoku remained still, unresponsive, their chest refusing to rise. The silence grew heavier as Finnegan's relentless effort tried to claw against the inevitability of loss itself. "Please," he cried.

"Fin." I tugged at his shoulder, but he pulled away from me. "Finnegan, that's enough." I pulled harder this time, tearing him from his friend as his hands hopelessly clung to Hoku's suit.

"I'm sorry," I said as Jones turned away, facing the ship.

"It's all my fault." Finnegan cried as I held him. Clinging to me as he sobbed, staring down at his friend.

"It's not your fault. Don't put that weight on your shoulders." I gripped him tighter, tears beginning to well in my own eyes.

I studied Hoku. Their eyes were closed in peaceful stillness, and their fur laid soft against their face. As my gaze wandered, something caught my attention. My eyes snapped back to Hoku as my breath hitched, unsure if it was a trick of my mind. But there it was again: a tiny, almost imperceptible, rise and fall of their chest. Hope burned through me.

"They're breathing." The words were barely a whisper as they left me, but Finnegan heard, turning to his friend.

Hoku's chest rose and fell once more, shallow and fragile. Their pointed ears twitched, but their eyes remained shut.

"Let's get them inside."

Jones cleared a small area on the floor as Finnegan and I carried Hoku over. We set them down gently before waiting to see them breathe again. Their breathing steadied as time passed, though it was still shallow. Finnegan stayed by their side, holding their hands, waiting for the moment they opened their eyes.

Jones changed her comms to only converse with mine so Finnegan couldn't hear. "We don't have any medical supplies."

I turned with a sigh, changing over my own comms. "I know."

"That was both reckless and dangerous. Why were they on top of the ship without rope? That was a close call and far too risky." The irritation in Jones's voice was palpable.

I sighed again. "If you happen to find any rope, let me know. As of right now, we're running on limited resources. Was it stupid? Yes, I don't disagree, but I'm also not going to shit on them for trying to get us the hell out of here. At this point our lives depend on the risks we're willing to take, and Hoku is a great climber. It was an improbable accident." Her exasperation was clear on her face. "You were scared we'd lost them too. All of us were."

She clenched her jaw, turning away. "I need you to come to the lab with me. I need help carrying some stuff back here." With that, she stood, storming down the dimly lit hall.

I took a moment to gaze at Finnegan and Hoku before following her.

Lest We Perish

Jonah 1:14

The lab was in utter ruin. Tiny glass vials, once neatly arranged along the walls, were shattered, their contents forming chaotic pools of sediment across the floor. Scattered notes and journals were soaked in chemicals and dirt, making their ink smear into illegible blots. The ceiling panels hung, jagged and warped, and the floor twisted underfoot. The air hung heavy with silent lament for the years' worth of painstaking research reduced to nothing more than a pile of useless rubble and wasted potential. A devastated look sat upon Jones's features as the corners of her lips turned down.

"What a mess," she said, studying the floor.

"This-this was almost a decade's worth of work." I bent down to pick up a small metallic rock, watching it crumble to dust between my fingers.

"No, not the lab." She put her head in her hands. "I'm talking about this situation. Stranded on some unknown planet with a broken ship, down a crew member, and no signal?" She looked at me, brows furrowed.

"Yeah, not the best circumstances," I replied. My feet pushed around the rubble as I walked farther into the lab.

Bits and pieces of glass sparkled in the light. "On a positive note, we're still alive."

She let out a hearty laugh that reverberated through the room. "And how much longer is that going to last?" She raised an eyebrow in question, her smile fading.

I let out a breath. "Forever the pessimist." I brushed off one of the tables, the dust wafting through the air in a revolving eddy and translucent cloud.

"In any case, we're going to need this." Jones retrieved a microscope from the wreckage, slapping away at the dust and debris that clung to it. "Let's see if we can find some slides, tubes, and disks that aren't completely worthless."

We navigated the wreckage with deliberate care, searching the chaos, moving over every detail so as not to miss anything. Shards of shattered glass shimmered in the dim light. Drawer panels were pried open with a faint groan of warped metal, revealing piles of fragmented disks.

As we rummaged through the piles, we came across a handful of miraculously whole disks, some slightly scratched or buffed, but otherwise fine. Strangely, we found the microscope slides mostly intact in the rubble, coated in dust, their glass providing a faint glow as they reflected the light from beneath the debris.

The test tubes were a bit harder to find. Those that had been stored in the cabinets had been thrown to the ground, their fragile thin glass splintered. I stood upright, stretching my back and limbs as stiffness began to creep in from being hunched over for too long. My eyes wandered along the walls where the test tubes from old missions had been, landing upon a group of four tubes resting precariously against each other.

My voice cut through the silence. "Do the tubes have to be sterile?"

"God, I wish. But we're not going to get anything sterile out of this." Jones stood and looked to where I pointed. "Those will work."

As her fingers reached for the test tubes teetering on the edge of the shelf, a scream shattered the air. A sound so chilling it seemed to vibrate through the metal walls, echoed in our ears. It wasn't human. It was raw, guttural, and feral. We froze, both of us staring toward the door.

My breath caught, my heartbeat loud in my ears, every fiber of my being screaming for me to run.

Jones moved to turn away, her pinky catching the slightest edge of the tubes. They rattled against each other in frozen hesitation as another echoing scream twisted and warped down the hallway.

I watched the tubes plummet to the ground, jagged shards of glass exploding outward.

"Shit!" Jones exclaimed as she rushed to check the tubes that now seamlessly blended in with the rest of the debris.

Another scream. This time it sounded like an amalgamation of hisses and roars tore through the air, sending shivers down my spine.

Jones held three tubes triumphantly in her hand. "Got a few. Let's go."

We raced down the halls, adrenaline forcing our legs to move as fast as they could carry us. Glass clinked together as our equipment jostled in our arms. My lungs burned as fear tugged at my mind.

As we dashed around the corner, my eyes widened in disbelief.

Hoku thrashed violently at the center of the bridge, their body a storm of flailing limbs. Their arms were driven in a chaotic, ravenous frenzy, each movement raw with desperation and fury. The guttural hisses and rapid clicks of their native tongue reverberated through the air, sharp tone fluctuations inhuman, climbing from their throat in a primal warning.

Frothy drool fell from their lips, the corners of their mouth bubbling with erratic streams in their feral state.

The rebreather. My eyes found it sitting in the rubble a few feet away as if tossed aside.

"What the hell is happening?" I asked without thinking.

Hoku's attention turned to me, crimson eyes glazed over in rage.

Shit.

Finnegan moved closer to Hoku, clutching his side, tears streaming down his face in fear as red dripped between his fingers. As Hoku began to advance, Finnegan grabbed them by the arm in a feeble attempt to stop them. Time slowed as I watched Hoku spin, fist connecting with Finnegan's helmet.

The impact echoed through the bridge, sending Finnegan hurtling back, his body skidding across the ground for several feet before coming to a jarring halt. Hoku bared sharp, pointed teeth as they sprinted to Finnegan, raining blow after blow upon his helmet as he lay curled into a ball.

Screams of terror echoed in my ears, and I was unable to wrap my mind around what was happening.

"Hoku, enough!" Jones yelled, rushing to Finnegan's aid, wrapping her arms around Hoku in a frail attempt to restrain them.

My legs moved on their own, grabbing Finnegan and dragging him to safety under my console. His breathing was shallow and quick, fear forcing his pupils into pinpricks as sweat beaded his forehead. I pressed his hand harder against the wound on his side, hoping the pressure would staunch the bleeding. There was no time to look for supplies or inspect the wound as Hoku flung Jones into the wall.

I have to stop them. In a flash, I tackled Hoku to the ground. I tried to pin their arms, but their strength was unparalleled. Their language chanted through my ears, growling words I couldn't recognize before my vision flipped. My gaze found the red flaky symbols lining the ceiling in what were supposed to be words of comfort and now seemed like anything but.

Hoku hoisted me into the air and drove me into the floor, the impact vibrating through my teeth. Alarms resounded from the speakers in my suit as pain flooded my body, only to intensify as Hoku slammed me down again. Over and over, I was hurled into the floor, my suit barely holding together as my oxygen tank began to cave. Pain shot down my spine every time I connected. My vision began to blur, my lungs losing air as my body begged for it to be over. *I'm going to die.*

Hoku stopped.

I paused to catch my breath and stall the alarms in my suit, then rolled over and pushed myself up. My gaze drifted to Jones first, our eyes connecting for a fleeting moment in shared agony. Determination held her jaw, her body tense.

My attention focused back on Hoku who had made their way back to the center of the bridge. Raspy hisses and clicks left their throat. Their claws raked across their face, blood tracing the wounds as they pulled at their eyes and teeth. Another blood-curdling and throaty scream expelled from their lungs.

I winced, watching as they slung their arms wildly through the air. They neared the console Finnegan was hidden under, red pooling along his suit.

"Hoku!" They ignored my call, instead leaning upon the console with both arms, staring down at it with terrified eyes. Hoku lifted their head and rammed it into the console with a sickening *crack*.

The console erupted in shattered glass and sparks as jagged shards rained around Finnegan. Blood smeared across the fractured surface as their skull continued to meet with the console.

Jones lifted a piece of scrap metal and swung at Hoku, landing a hit in their ribs with a bone crunching smack. Hoku stumbled, wailing.

I moved forward, unsure of what to do. Could I calm them down? *Would they even listen?*

"Hoku." My hands trembled as I drew closer, every fiber of my being against my actions. "Hoku, please." Before my outstretched hand could reach them, our bodies collided. We tumbled along the floor of the bridge before coming to a halt.

They pinned me as their fists rained upon my helmet, my visor desperately holding together. Hoku's punches weren't aimed, instead landing upon my chest, throat, and arms, anywhere they could reach.

I slapped at their tirade in a feeble attempt to deflect them. My right hand reached into the side pocket of my suit. My fingertips met with a hard metal surface as my legs kicked, trying to break free. As Hoku clasped both hands above their head, ready to strike my helmet again, my right arm swung.

Silence.

At first, all I could hear was the pounding of my pulse in my ears as I stared at what I had just done.

Hoku stared too, mouth agape, betrayal crawling over their features. Red began to stain my hand, soaking into the thirsty fibers of the suit. Ragged breaths escaped my lips as I let go of the knife still lodged in their throat.

Hoku's hands fell around my neck, their grip tightening in strained panic.

I pushed their face with one hand as my other tried frantically to peel their fingers away. Their body convulsed as blood poured from the wound in their neck, soaking my suit in a deep arterial red. Then, all at once, their body stopped.

I slipped away from their grasp, crawling across the floor, my eyes locked on the corpse of my once friend. *What the fuck?* Tears gathered behind my eyes as I shook, adrenaline hiding the pain I knew my bones were harboring.

"Cap." Jones's voice was small.

"I-I'm s-sorry," I croaked, my throat dry and words butchered. I pushed my head between my knees, rocking back and forth, desperately trying to calm down. *What have I done?* I felt a hand on my shoulder and turned to see Jones squatting next to me, her expression unreadable.

"It's okay." She removed her hand. "Are you hurt?"

I took a few more gulps of air, my vision blurring. I stared at Hoku's lifeless body. They lay motionless, crumpled awkwardly against the cold, rubble strewn ground. A dark crimson pool radiated slowly outward from their neck, a stark contrast against the pale metal of the knife. Their eyes stared blankly as hollow remnants of what used to be. The air around them grew heavy, laden with the chilling silence of what just transpired.

"No, nothing major," I replied. She nodded at my words. "You?"

"I'm good." Her attention turned to Finnegan, who still lay frozen under the console. I stood, stumbling my way to him with wobbling legs.

Finnegan's eyes were closed, and his skin was pale.

"Jones, see if there's anything we can patch his suit with nearby." My voice was raspy and strained.

She didn't respond, but I could hear her footsteps receding.

My gaze returned to Hoku, then down to my hands, stained red. *What have I done?*

Do Not Let It Spread

Leviticus 13:46

My head ached and my body felt sluggish. Every movement of my joints caused my muscles to groan in pain.

None of us managed to sleep last night. Jones and I had scrounged up some tape from the lab and hastily packed Finnegan's wound with crumpled papers and journal entries. The injury was brutal, an uneven gash running along his side, courtesy of one of Hoku's claws.

When Finnegan was able to move again, he avoided Hoku's body altogether, steering clear with deliberate shakes of his head, refusing even a fleeting glance in their direction.

Digging through the wreckage of the ship, I unearthed a torn piece of tarp and used it as a makeshift shroud, hiding Hoku from all of us. Little pieces of rubble decorated the outline of their body, like some dystopian silhouette.

Morale was down. Instead of the hopeful air floating through the dead ship, it was as if a heavy cloud had wrapped itself around each of us, fogging our minds.

Jones hadn't moved from her console in hours, staring down at both it and her holo, hoping for a glimmer of information, some sort of understanding. Finnegan lay against the wall by his console, the transmitter perched in his lap as he typed away at his holo.

I stared, trying to justify my previous actions. A tear threatened to fall down my cheek as I looked at my blood-stained suit, the same color as the paint along the ceiling. The silence enveloped me, suffocating as guilt-trodden fingers gripped at my lungs and throat.

"Should we say something?"

I jumped at the sound of her voice. I hadn't noticed Jones next to me, nor Finnegan behind. Her voice was solemn, her expression dark and stoic.

I could see why people willingly followed her into battle. In the face of disaster, she still held an air of calm and power around her shoulders, her head held high.

"No," Finnegan replied, "they wouldn't hear it anyways." He winced as he limped away, the wound impeding his movement.

I sighed. *What would I even say?*

"May the universe guide you home, Hoku." Jones's voice wavered against the words. A lump formed in my own throat. "May you find peace among the wreckage of our ship, our home."

I gazed at her for a moment, the weight of the situation sharpening her features and dulling her eyes. This wasn't the first time she'd done this. Her words were spoken with practiced familiarity, as though the burial of her peers had become routine. Having led a rebel force, it could only be assumed she had buried one too many friends.

We stood in silence, letting the world wash over us as the feeling of despair grew with each passing minute. It was heavy, weakening my spirit and knees.

I turned to see Finnegan, once again slumped along the wall, holo in hand. The cold blue light of the screen washed over his sullen features. He looked exhausted. His normally red curly hair that bounced around his glasses seemed to droop around him, falling into his eyes and around his ears, hiding them away. His eyes were glazed over, the code on the screen drifting along the surface of his glasses completely unseen. *Shit.*

I made my way over to him. He didn't look up or react as I slid down the wall next to him. "How's it going?" I asked. He gave me a sideways glance. "The coding?" I nodded my head toward his holo.

He shrugged.

I turned my gaze away, focusing on the ship instead. In the chaos of the crash, I hadn't taken the time to truly assess the damage. Now, however, as I scanned the remains of our ship, whatever fragile hope I still possessed crumbled.

The entire midsection looked as if it had been crushed and twisted upon impact. The bottom half of the ship containing the engines and cargo was completely buried and crushed into the ground. Warped metal folding in on itself like ragged scrap filled every corner and wall. The mess hall was barely recognizable. Instead, a gaping hole of blackened and torn away steel sat where the dining table once stood. Only a single chair remained, its frame grotesquely contorted and legs bent at unnatural angles.

The kitchen wasn't any better. Cabinets and supplies had been ripped away, their remains scattered upon the ground. Broken tree limbs had splintered and pierced through the metal, driving deep into the wreckage. The ship's walls were battered and broken, their once smooth surfaces cracked and fractured, exposing a tangle of frayed wires and ruptured pipes, as if it's very guts had been wrenched open, spilling out in a disgusting display of devastation. Our home had been demolished.

"It's a mess, isn't it?" I shook my head as the words fell from my mouth. Finnegan gave a fleeting glance to the ship surrounding us. He shrugged again, the rustling of his suit loud against his sudden vow of silence. "It's been a long time since we've been in shit this deep, right?"

My words met with silence still, and I looked to my hands. The blood had dried and become a russet copper, filling in the tiny divots between the dark fibers of my gloves. I ran my fingers over it, watching how it flaked off, tumbling through the air and settling with the dust and debris on the ground. It reminded me of the words Hoku had so carefully painted along our ceiling.

"I'm sorry." My voice was steady but my feelings wavered. An unwelcome, somber blanket fell upon my shoulders. It was unbearably heavy.

"For what?" Finnegan's voice barely broke through the fog of my thoughts.

I sighed, leaning my head back against the wall, my eyes meeting with the flaking paint meant to protect us. "About Hoku."

"It's fine." The words fell flat. We both knew he didn't mean them. "You did what you had to."

My gaze traced the symbols and words until they landed upon the tarp-laden body, the bits of debris preserving it from sight. A small grave in the ruins of the ship.

"It's not," I said, shaking my head, feeling the trembling of my fingers. I wrung my hands together, more blood chipping off. "I know what it's like to lose someone."

Finnegan exhaled sharply, rubbing a hand along his visor. "I don't want to talk about this." He waved a hand in dismissal, but it lacked conviction, falling limp.

I hesitated.

"I really am sorry," I said, softer this time. "Hoku's never acted like that. It just felt . . . wrong."

Finnegan let out a bitter laugh, a forlorn smile tugging at his lips. "Wrong doesn't even begin to describe it." His voice cracked at the edge of the words, but he caught himself. "One minute we're laughing and goofing off. The next they're trying to kill me. I'm just, I don't know." He cut himself off, his jaw tightening. His hand brushed over the makeshift bandage at his side, eyes growing distant.

I wasn't sure what to say, preferring to let the quiet comfort both of us for a moment. Watching the way tears gathered and glistened in the corners of Finnegan's eyes, I felt a twinge in my chest.

"We were best friends," he said as he placed his head in his hands, his gloves slipping along the helmet's surface. "We survived that shithole prison together. We shared our languages with each other." His voice caught, tears streaming down his face, plummeting to the bottom of his visor.

"You guys shared a lot of life."

"It's not just that. We watched each other's backs and fought together. Every day for years. Stuck in that stupid prison, with those stupid guards. I got them through the torture Revanche put them through. I was there for them through *everything*."

I felt my heart growing heavy. He blew out a breath before continuing.

"I promised we'd make it out of Revanche together. We brought each other peace when shit like this—" A soft hiccup pulled at his lungs. "But I didn't even recognize them in the end."

I put a comforting hand on his shoulder, trying to help bear the weight he carried.

"I keep thinking," his voice was raspy now, clawing through his throat against the swell of emotion. "If I just hadn't made them climb on top of the ship, if I had found another way, if I hadn't been so stupidly hasty. Maybe this wouldn't have happened."

I swallowed against the lump in my throat. "It's not your fault."

"Sure feels like it," he said. He let out a slow breath, staring just past the tarp his friend lay beneath.

"I can't convince you otherwise," I said. "Though, they would never blame you."

He nodded in response. "I know."

I pursed my lips as we sat together, letting the silence sit heavy against our words. But this time, the weight was between the both of us. Though it was uncomfortable, it was a little bit easier to bear, and I could see the way Finnegan's shoulders had begun to relax as he collected himself.

"Hey, I know this is probably the last thing you want to do right now, but let's work on getting that transmitter up and running, yeah?" I said, nudging him with my elbow. *There is barely time to grieve.*

I focused on letting my body become numb to the constant onslaught of emotion I'd been feeling for the last few hours, shouldering the weight of Finnegan's pain and my own and holding strong. "I'll climb up there, and you tell me what to do, finish what you guys started, and get the hell out of here. How does that sound?"

Finnegan sucked in a breath, drawing his legs in to stand up. "Yeah, let's get Hoku back home."

Outside, my eyes were assaulted once more with vivid colors of this unforgiving and unfamiliar world. I clenched my teeth while my arms cried out in pain as I climbed to the top of the ship, the metal beneath my body groaning under my weight. My foot slipped from its hold, and my heart skipped a beat as my muscles strained to catch myself. *Shit.*

I reached the top and caught my breath, a worried anxiousness settling in my stomach.

I felt all hope leave my body as I stared out at the scenery before me. The height of the trees was astounding. Even from the top of our ship, I had to crane my neck upward to make out the deep red of the canopy above. Even more damning was the size of the forest itself. It was so immense, it blocked my sight in every direction. The expansive purple and red wall surrounded us on all sides, completely encasing.

Our ship was in far worse condition than I previously thought. A scorched trail of torn metal flanked by the jagged and broken remains of tree trunks led straight to us.

Our ship. It had carved a clearing into the forest, the split and shattered remains of tree trunks leaving behind red and purple leaves like blood splattering from their vicious mauling.

The ship itself was a hollowed out husk of twisted and beaten metal. The ship was almost unrecognizable. Besides the main bridge and part of our eastern side, everything was demolished. Large scrapes and tears clawed along the metal, exposing wires and pipes. Soot and ash from the fires of the crash covered the environment in a smoky, stained blanket.

I felt the familiar pull of anxiety knotting my stomach and closing my throat. Tearing my eyes away from the wreckage, I was met once more with the enormous trees. They completely dwarfed our ship. I felt small and insignificant as I watched the limbs and leaves.

They made no motion. The limbs dared not touch or intertwine, with no wind to rustle their leaves and, it seemed, no animals to play among the branches.

Isolated.

"Do you see the wire?" Finnegan's voice pierced through the speakers in my suit.

I looked down at him. He looked so tiny on the ground, much smaller than he already was.

I gave a quick thumbs up before pulling the transmitter from the back of my suit where we'd attached it with pieces of scavenged wire.

"Cut it," I said as I began untangling the cables of the transmitter. The power to the ship faltered, giving a sputtering gasp as though struggling to breathe. The dim lights that remained flickered and died before leaving a dark emptiness behind. The power shutting off released a cascading symphony of mechanical failures: sharp clicks as door locks gave way, dull thunks as relays disengaged, and then . . . nothing.

Silence, even deeper than before, absorbed the ambient sounds we had originally ignored.

My skin prickled and my hair rose. My hands fumbled as I removed the outside shell of the auxiliary wire. There was no promise that the power would return. No assurance the transmitter wouldn't fry in the process. No certainty we wouldn't be stranded here, powerless, and left to starve. There was no guarantee we'd make it out alive.

The wire consisted of several layers. First the braided shielding, a tight weave of metallic composite strands that provided additional protection against physical damage. Beneath that, the insulation layer gleamed in the light, helping protect the wire from extreme conditions and electromagnetic interference. Then it was the core. Copper and silver wires wove together in large braids, still warm to the touch even through the gloves of my suit. The transmitter wires were much smaller, less protected versions of that same wire where small bits of insulation had fused and melted.

I stripped away the charred casing, exposing the raw wire within. Sweat beaded along my brow as I spliced the lines together, the exposed copper and silver twisting in my hands like a tangle of nerves. A thin wisp of smoke curled up in the air as they connected. It wasn't elegant, more like a butcher's work than an electrician's. The wires bulged grotesquely from the hasty tangle of tape wrapped around it.

"Bring it back to life." My voice was sick with worry. I stepped back, jaw clenched, waiting to see if the jerry-rigged connection would hold or if it would explode in a sea of sparks.

Finnegan's voice wasn't much steadier than mine. "Bringing it back."

A low hum resonated through the walls, faint at first but quickly swelling as the ship reawakened. Lights flickered hesitantly, casting wild shadows before stabilizing. The few working consoles we had left flared to life, displays pulsing. Sparks began to drop from hanging and exposed wires once more, like little stars in the dim interior of the bridge. The transmitter let out a sharp beep as its green light began flashing. I held my breath for a moment, waiting for it to erupt in flames, but it didn't. It sat still on the roof of the ship.

"Good to go," I said as I exchanged glances with Finnegan down below, both of us wide-eyed and breathless as cautious hope began to dawn.

My heart beat with renewed vigor as I made my descent to the ground, the transmitter strapped to my back.

"This is the first bit of good news yet." Jones sighed in relief.

"Things are looking up." I nodded, taking a moment to relax by leaning against the wall inside the bridge.

Finnegan wasted no time, pulling the transmitter from my back and lengthening the wire so it didn't catch on broken panels. He poured over his holo and console, dedicated to finding a way to boost the signal.

"I'm still worried." Jones's voice was a whisper this time. She had changed her comms to only relay through my suit again.

I stole a look at Finnegan who was fully immersed in his holo.

She gave me a distressed glance. "Come look at this."

As we approached her console, data spilled across the cracked screen in a wild tapestry of numbers, graphs, and shifting molecular structures. The chemical analysis appeared first, long arrays of spectral peaks and elemental breakdowns, glowing in sharps hues, each element tagged with a pulsing icon. A DNA readout unfurled in a digital helix as the screen split, rendering the helix into two sections, each strand glowing faintly as the base pairs aligned and twisted, each nucleotide a distinct color in the kaleidoscope of genetic information.

Annotative notes on mutational probabilities and biochemical interactions scrolled rapidly down one side, detailed in Jones's handwriting. Every few seconds the console beeped softly, updating with new results.

"What am I looking at?" I kept my voice low.

"I want to preface this by saying you're not going to like what I had to do." My brow furrowed at her words as she tapped away at the screen. "Hoku's DNA was modified. It mutated quickly. Their entire inner biology changed and erupted into something else. I—"

My brow furrowed. "What did you do?"

She hesitated, studying me for a moment before sighing. "Hoku's DNA was modified from the inside out. It mutated rapidly. Their entire biology was being broken down and reformed."

"Hold on." I cut her off with a raise of my hand. "What did you do?"

Her expression softened, but she didn't look guilty, just tired. "I analyzed a sample of their blood and brain tissue while you and Finnegan were busy with the transmitter."

I felt my stomach drop. "You what?"

"I had to." Her voice was quiet, barely audible through the speakers in my helmet. "They were decomposing too quickly. I needed to understand what was happening before—"

"Damn it, Jones." My voice shook in hushed anger. "When I said analyze everything, I didn't mean desecrate our dead friend." I glared at her in disgust, my mouth slightly agape. But she met my eyes, her jaw tightening.

"Listen, I understand how it sounds, but in case you didn't notice, Hoku went from friend to foe in a matter of hours." She crossed her arms. "I needed to know why. In case you also haven't noticed, their body is decomposing at an alarmingly unnatural rate. None of that concerns you?"

I clenched my teeth but said nothing. She returned her attention to the screen. We remained in heavy silence for a moment.

"Mutations?" I finally asked.

She nodded. "Something unknown entered their bloodstream. These tiny cells here,"—she gestured at the display—"at first I thought they were a virus. Except they're not like anything I've ever seen before. That is, until I took a closer look."

The screen flickered as a small video played from the microscope work she had done. Fluffy, white, cell-like structures with spiked walls moved about the blood cells, barely an eighth of their size. But they quickly surrounded the blood cells, draining them and taking over. They moved rapidly, swarming each cell and pushing their spikes as deep as they could go.

"What are they?" I asked.

"They remind me of entomopathogenic fungi," she said.

"English, please."

She rolled her eyes in response, still leaning over the console. "A microscopic fungus that attacks insects by penetrating their exoskeleton and releasing toxins." She shook her head.

"So, for bugs?"

"Except *we're* the bugs." She held up a vial of thick black sludge. "It's able to immediately overcome any remaining immune response and breaks down the body once it's inside to fuel itself."

I reeled back in disgust.

"This is what's left." She set the vial down. "What the inside of the body becomes."

There was a pause as we digested the information. I felt bile rising in my throat.

"It creates these tiny, microscopic structures, like the spores from fungus back on Earth. Though at home, once the spore stalks appear, the entire body has already been colonized," she murmured, watching in awe. "The pathogen mutates so quickly the immune system can't keep up, even when it does finally recognize the threat."

A slow creeping terror began to settle around me.

Jones kept going. "Even more fascinating is, once it's inside the host cells, it can replicate without an issue, essentially hiding in plain sight." She shook her head. "Though that acts more like a virus and less like a fungus."

I swallowed hard. "Maybe it's some kind of hybrid?"

"Maybe." Her voice trailed off as she studied the console, the data streaming along her visor in a frenzy.

"Where do they come from? Are they just airborne?" I questioned, still confused.

"I don't know." She exhaled sharply. "They're so small, they could be anywhere. If they're spores like fungus, it's possible it's reserved to spreading through the wind or touch. If it's a virus, it could be bodily fluids."

"Then we prepare for the worst," I said. "We act like it's covering every inch of this planet."

"I do know one thing." She looked at me expectantly. "Once they're in, they're in. They move quickly through the blood stream. But even more fascinating is how they affected the brain."

"Fascinating?" I raised an eyebrow at her as I crossed my arms.

A small smile tugged at the corners of her lips before she pursed them, her fingers gliding across the console. "Here."

A video began displaying the analysis of the brain tissue she had fed into the machine. Similar microscopic cells emerged, writhing through the fatty tissue with invasive tendrils. They stretched and twisted, latching on to nerves and intertwining them in a grotesque dance of mutation, merging into a hideous new structure.

"It's taking over." My heartbeat was loud in my ears, my breath taken from my lungs. Panic began to wind its hands through my body.

"It is." She cleared her throat. "It completely rewires the brain. I don't know what purpose this would serve other than to try and assimilate or control whatever life form happens to land here. It's the same cells, but they react differently to blood and brain cells."

"If it attacks the brain like that . . ." My voice trailed off as my eyes snapped to Finnegan.

His skin had become sickly pale with a sheen of sweat shining in the dim light of his holo. His breathing was shallow, his chest barely moving as his lungs tried to expand, and his eyes were red in the corners, irritated and dry.

"That's why I wanted to talk to you." She had followed my gaze, her voice cautious. "I don't know how long he has, but if this thing is already in his system, it's too late."

I went to pinch the bridge of my nose, but my fingers thumped against my visor. I sighed, closing my eyes while I tried to think.

We couldn't lose Finnegan too. It was imperative he stayed alive to get a signal out. He was the only one who understood the tech enough to do so. The few times he'd taught me bits and pieces of coding wouldn't serve us all that well.

"We can't lose him." My voice was firm but the words were empty.

"I don't think—"

"He's fine. We're going to make it out of this. He's going to send the signal, people are going to come and rescue us, and—" I felt a hand on my shoulder.

A forlorn look settled against Jones's features. "Cap."

"No." My voice was sharp. "We, as in all of us, are making it out of this hellhole. We just need rest. You'll have time tomorrow to run all the tests you want. Hell, analyze Finnegan's progression if you have to."

"We don't have time." She flung her arms in exasperation, turning away from me, gripping the console. "In case you haven't noticed, we're all running low on oxygen. We have no food. No water. The rebreather is now a last resort, not a solution. It's *over*."

I let out a frustrated breath. "Here we go again with the pessimism." My hands curled into fists at my side. "We've haven't survived every shitstorm the universe has thrown at us for this fucking deserted planet to win. We are not dying here."

"Maybe for you there's a chance." Her voice echoed through my helmet as she winced at her own words.

"What do you mean?" My voice was shallow, my throat dry.

She held up the vial once more. Inside, the thick black sludge sloshed against the glass. Hoku's name was scrawled across it. "Remember how I said once it's in, it's over?"

"Jones."

"It's over for me." She lifted her arm, a small patch of tape glinting in the crook.

"No." My heart sank. "No way."

She forced a weak smile. "My suit must've torn when we were grappling Hoku. I only noticed it a few hours ago." She swallowed hard. "I've already been exposed."

I stared at the console, watching the video play on repeat, the tendril-like arms of the cells attaching themselves to nerves.

My mind scrambled for anything to prove she wasn't infected. "Hoku changed in a few hours, and you're fine right now, right? So, maybe there's a second trigger, or maybe it's not in the air, right? Maybe it's not too late."

"I-I'm not really sure," she stammered.

I latched on to that uncertainty with a viselike grip. "Then we'll figure it out in the morning. You can study it then. We're all tired and need to get some rest." With that, I turned away, moving toward my console, changing my comms back to be heard by everyone.

I didn't want to think about it. I couldn't think about it. Both Jones and Finnegan had been exposed to whatever happened to Hoku, and yet both seemed fine so far? I couldn't wrap my head around it.

Jones had made swift progress, but we needed to know more. The images from her console haunted me, flashing in my mind like a warning I couldn't escape. Those cells, devouring the brain sample, swarming like predators through the blood, moved with such purpose, such malice.

My stomach churned as my hands trembled. I wanted Jones to keep pushing, to keep searching, but what choice did we have? We were exhausted, dehydrated, and starving. Each one of us was fraying at the edges. We needed to rest, even if every fiber of my being screamed that we shouldn't.

My integrity almost collapsed when my body hit the floor. My muscles ached and my mind burned. I was losing control. Tears pricked at the back of my eyes as I set my head in my hands.

It's over. Jones's words rang in my ears.

How could this happen?

Divine punishment had never felt so cruel.

The Blood of The Innocent

Matthew 27:4

Sleep came in brief, restless waves. At night, the corpse of our metal ship became icy, its hard surface unyielding against our aching bodies. We tried to huddle close, desperate for warmth, while our breath fogged our visors, condensing into a chill that seeped deeper into our suits. Even space didn't feel this cold.

The gnarled and ugly hands of nightmares clawed their way into me, grotesque and relentless, dragging me back to the pain and chaos of everything that had happened after the crash. Their twisted fingers gripped at my thoughts, refusing to let go, forcing me to relive every harrowing moment.

This time when I woke, sweat pooled along my back and forehead. The inky darkness surrounding us was suffocating. Large, threatening shadows blanketed the walls, consuming even the faintest light.

I sat up, groggy, feeling my stiff muscles sting with the effort. My eyes wandered lazily to the alien sky outside the ship. I was just barely able to see the bottom half of one of the moons, its verdant surface still in pastoral silence as it stared back.

I closed my eyes, mind drifting as I sat, feeling the weight of hushed peace around me. Then small whispers filled my ears, staticky and muffled. My brow furrowed as

I tilted my head, trying to focus. The whispers were faint, coming through the helmet's speakers in sparing intervals. I turned slowly, my wearied eyes barely making out the figure before me.

Finnegan stood deeper in the ship, by the broken walls and cabinets of the kitchen, head pressed against the wall. A chill wound up my spine as my heart began to race.

"Fin?" His name caught in my dry throat.

Finnegan didn't move, but my breath hitched as I realized his helmet was gone. It lay several feet away, glinting in the starlight like some discarded omen. Scattered between us were strands of copper hair, torn violently from the roots, like a grim breadcrumb trail leading to him.

My legs wobbled as I forced myself to stand, the sight of him pulling another tuft of hair from his head churning my stomach. Through the speakers of my suit, his voice poured in as a stream of incoherent, feverish whispers. My skin crawled, my mind wavering. I took a few halfhearted steps toward him, the static fading.

"They don't get it. They never will." His head twitched to the side, hands clawing at his face. "Listen to me, they don't get it."

Fear took hold of me as he slammed his hands into his head and the wall, aggression fueling his movements. Tension built in my joints as I inched forward.

"Fin?" My voice was barely audible, caught against the lump in my throat.

Jones rustled behind me, the sound of her suit against the ground my only solace.

"You." Fin pulled his head from the wall, stopping the onslaught of his hands. "You. You did this. You." He stopped. He moved his head to watch me from the corner of his eye.

I froze, unsure of what to do.

"What're you guys doing?" Jones's voice was disoriented and raspy as she woke.

"I can't keep doing this." Finnegan's lips curved into a slow, unsettling smile as his eyes locked on mine. A sort of sad desperation filled his eyes, as if in defeat. "They always find me, no matter how I crunch the numbers. My debt is unpaid."

His words sank into me like ice, leaving me confused and grasping desperately for a response. Before I could utter a word, he bolted, slipping through the door and melting into the shadows. Instinct took over, and I lunged after him, my pulse hammering in my ears.

Jones called behind me, but I didn't stop to listen. My lungs heaved as I pushed forward, sprinting through the rubble of our ship. The darkness swelled in every direction, pushing in on all sides, but I fixed on the faint glint of light catching what was left of Finnegan's hair. My legs hopelessly tried to close the gap between us. Every breath seared in my chest, my body screaming for rest. But I kept going, the crumbling ship becoming a jagged maze.

Our footsteps pounded against the warped metal of the floor, echoing through the desolate halls. Torn panels jutted out like spiked teeth, while sparks from severed wires cast fleeting shadows, offering barely enough light to see.

I stumbled into the middle of the ship and stopped, gasping for air. I doubled over, my hands braced on my knees. A warning flickered orange at the edge of my helmet's display: *Oxygen Low.* Panic settled along my skin, but then I saw it.

My blood chilled as I squinted in the dim light. Spatters of red painted the floor ahead, each drop rough and uneven, stretching into sharp-tailed streaks, and leading deeper into the darkness.

Jones's footsteps echoed behind me.

"It was over the minute I sent it out." Finnegan stepped out of the shadows. The gloom surrounded his tired sunken eyes and hollow cheeks. His features were sharper in the dim light, crooked and honed. "Secrets are never truly hidden, but you know that better than anyone, right Cap?" His eyes flicked to mine, dull and glazed over.

"I don't know what you're talking about." My voice shook, and my head pounded for lack of air.

He let out a hearty laugh before stopping abruptly. "Liar," he spat.

I tried to see deeper into the darkness, but there was nothing there.

"Finnegan, I don't know what's going on."

"Shut up!" he snapped. "No, you can't. You don't understand." He shook his head, whispering to the empty air beside him.

I looked at Jones who shrugged, looking just as tired and confused as I felt.

I sighed, taking a few uncertain steps toward him. "Fin, you're not making any sense." My voice was steady, filled with worry and endearment.

Finnegan's head snapped up to face us, jaw clenched and eyes wide.

Jones reached out, Finnegan's helmet in her hands. "You should put this back on."

"Don't get any closer," he growled. "Get away!" He began to thrash as he retreated into the shadows, dull thuds echoing through the room as his limbs hit debris and the metal floor.

Jones and I rushed into the darkness, trying to find him as the noises grew louder. I watched in horror, as his body thrashed against the ground in a pool of chemicals from the ship's broken pipes, ripples and splashes flying in a shimmering, multicolored wash. The serrated edges of metal panels tore into his suit and skin, leaving stains of red to mix with the volatile runoff.

I waded to him, grabbing his arms as he flailed. He was slick with greasy sludge, and my hands lost their grip.

A scream bubbled up from his throat, choked and wet as it tore through the air. It was an unending and unholy sound that vibrated in our bones. He gasped for air only to continue the splitting wail as he swung his body erratically.

Jones helped by grabbing his legs, but Finnegan gave a swift kick to her helmet before slipping from my grasp.

"Wait!" I lost my balance, the world tilting as I crashed to the ground. The sludge around me blinded my view.

Jones pulled me up, my body gnawing with pain as we moved in pursuit of our friend.

The ship became a maze of rubble the farther we delved, but Finnegan left us with an easy trail of grease and gargled screams to follow. We moved through the obstacle course, contorting our bodies to fit through small gaps of sheared metal walls and crushed doors. We grew anxious as we moved, the flickering overhead lights barely alive from what was left of the auxiliary power.

Shit. It was dizzying. I felt lost. The ship was too dark, too unfamiliar.

Jones put a hand on my arm. "We should stop."

"We can't." I pushed her hand away.

"We're just causing him to hurt himself more. We should try to find him in the morning," Jones responded, still following me through the ship.

It burned. Everything burned. My body and my mind felt like they were on fire. Wild, out of control flames licked at every surface of my being and yet I was cold. I wasn't in control anymore. I was just a puppet being strung along for the ride.

"He's the only one who can send a signal out. We need him."

"We can't—"

"I'm not abandoning him to go through this alone." I glared at her. "We see this through."

Sliding between another set of splintered doors, we made our way into what used to be the southern end of the ship. Its maw yawned open before us, a cavernous wound carved deep into its metallic flesh. The broken edges of the breach were gross, bent and twisted outward as if the ship had been violently disemboweled. Blackened scars left streaks along the torn metal and shredded wiring hung like sinew, unmoving in the cold air.

The sky beyond the wreck was just beginning to lighten, but the faint glow only deepened my sense of dread. The light cast long shadows that crawled over the fractured floor and glinted off the shattered hold, painting the scene a pale, sickly hue. The interior was shrouded in shadow, the faint light revealing a chaotic tangle of collapsed beams and warped panels that twisted in and out of the walls before disappearing into nothingness.

I approached the obliterated area, my breath catching at the scale of destruction. It was a pitiless, open grave for our hopes of survival.

The silence was unnerving. My steps faltered as I stared into the darkness that beckoned with quiet malice. Despair wrapped around my heart, heavy and unrelenting, as I realized just how little of the ship remained and how much of us it had already consumed. Then I saw it. A flash of glinting light fleeting across my eyes, too quick to focus on. I looked up, my stomach dropping.

Finnegan stood above the wreckage. His feet shifted slightly on the unsteady surface of broken cargo boxes. Wires framed him as the light from the sky created a back glow, hiding his face. Just before him, the floor had collapsed, exposing the ship's lower level. The edges of the hole curled inward, warped metal and torn wiring hanging like severed veins. The basement cargo hold yawned beneath, a black void waiting to swallow whatever strayed too close. Frantic cries and whispers made their way through the air but remained indecipherable until his voice rose to echo through the room.

"Help." Finnegan let one foot hang over the edge. "Please. Help me." His voice sounded raw and pained, as if he'd been crying for hours.

"Fin, be careful!" Jones rushed past me, but I didn't dare move, holding my breath. Fear and unease settled under my skin as my chest burned, my mind losing its grip.

More whispers filled the air as Fin's body twitched, limbs moving at odd angles as the metal beneath his feet groaned. "I didn't mean to do it. I swear. I'm sorry. I didn't know it would go that far." Sobs racked his small frame.

"It's okay Fin, just come down. We'll patch you up." I tried to sound reassuring, my voice anything but.

"This isn't how it was supposed to go," Finnegan said. The erratic motions of his body stilled.

I watched, mouth agape as time seemed to stretch, a frozen fragment etching itself into my mind. Finnegan's foot continued to dangle over the edge for a tantalizing moment before his body tumbled forward, arms and legs getting caught in the tangle of wires surrounding him, twisting and jerking him in all directions.

I lunged instinctively, a yell tearing from my throat, lost in the hollow silence. Sickening snaps resounded as his bones broke from the mess of wires like hideous hands desperately trying to catch him.

For an instant, I saw his face, illuminated eyes glazed over in fear as he hopelessly clawed at the wires, gravity relentless. The metal walls of the wreckage rushed past him, the dim glow highlighting streaks of blood where his suit had been cut.

There was no sound as he fell, only the echoing *snap* as his neck caught one of the wires that refused to give under his weight. The noise reverberated through the hollow ship in a grim punctuation.

I froze, the emptiness in my chest mirroring the void Finnegan was frozen in. Silence returned, suffocating and absolute. I staggered toward him on unsteady legs, the jagged contours of twisted steel bathed in the pale light, my stomach churning as reality began to sink in.

He's gone. Swallowed by the ruins of the ship. This cursed planet had claimed another.

The Tower of Babel

Genesis 11:4

*U*nbelievable.

Finnegan's body hung in a twisted mess in the air, the breaking daylight illuminating his mangled form. I felt numb, as if my body weren't my own. I swallowed, but my throat felt like sandpaper, the iron taste of blood spreading across my tongue. I took a breath as my mind replayed Finnegan's death over and over.

His arms and legs stuck out in unnatural directions, bones jutting from the thick fabric of the suit, blood mixing with grease as it soaked into the fibers.

Jones knelt near the hole his body hung over, gently smoothing the debris along the ground. "May you find peace in your final rest." Her voice shook with grief. "Allow the stars to cleanse you on your journey home."

She lifted her head slowly as she placed his helmet in front of her, a soft thunk setting it into place. Her eyes remained dark as she handled her emotions, her expression grim. The light of day cascaded through the room, stretching its gentle hands through the disturbing scene of ragged metal and blood, bathing it in quiet comfort.

Tired. Exhausted. Drained. I felt completely numb. Everything was hopeless. We weren't surviving, just prolonging our inevitable deaths. Whatever happened with

Hoku and Finnegan would surely happen to us, and if it didn't, we were going to starve or die of thirst. There's no way to win.

Grief's cold hands tangled around my bones and throat, suffocating and silencing my thoughts. I wanted to mourn, but not just our losses. The situation, the future. Waves of emotion crashed over me, but my body wouldn't react.

Instead, my eyes remained glued to my friend strangled above me whose visor shined bits of light upon their face from the floor. Unrecognizable.

Jones stood, turning to face me, her lips pursed. "We should head back."

"We're just going to leave him?" I motioned to the body, my voice shockingly steady.

She turned back, and a long pause filled the air as she contemplated. "Let the sun continue to bathe him in innocence. It's not like we'd be able to retrieve him safely anyways."

She began to walk away, brushing her hand on my shoulder as she passed.

I continued to observe the scene before me. It would be beautiful if it didn't harbor death.

The gaping hole in the ship's hull stretched wide, its jagged edges silhouetted against the faint blush of early light spilling into the void. Through the breach, the vibrantly colored planet took hold, vast and ancient, its colors smearing the horizon in hues of bruised violets and deep reds. The air was thin as lazy trails of fog crept in, as if ghost-like breaths slipped between the shards of what was once whole. A lavender haze sat at the edges of my vision, delicate as it outlined the destruction in such a way that almost felt tender and soft.

Finnegan remained still, his face turned toward the light as if surrendering to its embrace. The blood that pooled below him in the basement cargo hold shimmered faintly, resembling the black sludge Jones had pulled from Hoku.

The sight should be unbearable, yet it held a strange grace I couldn't explain. I peeled my eyes away, stealing one more glance at the profoundly sickening scene transformed impossibly into something beautiful.

A chill fell over me as I made my way back to the bridge. The ship remained quiet. There was no sound, just oppressive silence so heavy it pressed against my skin. The wreckage, the death, the cold.

My head began to hurt as I walked and crawled through the walls of the ship, my feet shuffling forward, trembling. What if we hadn't landed here? What if Jones and I are already infected? What if . . .

I shook my head to dispel the thoughts. Thinking in what ifs wasn't going to get me anywhere. Figuring out how to survive was the important part. We needed to get a signal out. Finnegan and I got the transmitter working. I just needed to finish what we started. Jones could continue studying the planet. If anyone could understand what happened to the other two it would be her.

Upon reaching the bridge, the late morning sun cast short shadows across the floor while broken glass sparkled in the new light. My gaze fell upon Hoku's body, still protected from sight by the tarp and stones. If only . . .

I blinked slowly as I turned to find Jones hunched over her console, tapping away at the screen in obvious distress.

"Any good news?" My voice was hoarse. Neither of us have had water since the crash, nor had we managed to find any more food.

"No, we're fucked." She slammed a fist against the console, the glass giving way with a sharp crack. She let out an exasperated sigh.

I made my way to the wall by Finnegan's console. "We're just hungry and tired." I slumped down to the floor. The transmitter's blinking green light seemed more daunting than hopeful. Finnegan's holo lay next to me, the smooth glass and blue light reflecting the statuesque trees of the outside planet.

"Do you think they're looking for us?" Her voice was soft through my helmet. I almost wanted to ignore the question, to pretend I didn't hear. "No," I answered honestly.

"Why not?" Her voice was hoarse as her eyes remained glued to the console, the reflection of numbers and chemical compounds flying across her visor. "We've been the best crew Revanche has ever seen. We've brought them so much fucking money. We've done everything right."

"Why would they want to search for a lost ship of criminals?" I responded in a dull tone. "They cast us out like trash and sent us out on this shoddy flying piece of shit trying to catch ghosts. Do you really think they care? You think they'd lose even a single second of sleep over us vanishing from their precious radar?"

As I looked back down at the green blinking light, I felt something inside of me snap. The light's steady rhythm gnawed at me. Its pulsing indifference felt mocking, and frustration burned hot in my chest, tangling with the sharp sting of annoyance. I clenched my fists, the need to survive writhing in me like an unkempt worm.

This stupid transmitter, this flickering useless light, dangling a shred of hope I knew better than to trust. What was the point? The transmitter provided nothing but a false sense of security, making us the butt end of a cruel joke.

A lump burned in my throat as I watched the green fade in and out, like a countdown, daring me to try and fail. I ground my teeth as I resisted the urge to slam my fist into it, as though breaking it would somehow make me feel better. But no, it would only leave me with more pieces to try fitting back together while the universe watched and laughed.

"Who's being pessimistic now?" Jones continued to face the console, but I caught the faint smile that tugged at her lips like a flicker of light in a storm. Slowly, the building resentment that had taken residence in my chest began to ease.

I'm not alone.

We could still do this. There was still time.

"I'm sorry," I murmured, my voice raw and unfamiliar.

"Don't be sorry. Get to work on that transmitter." She looked up, meeting my gaze with a new, unshakable resolve. "We won't let their deaths be in vain." Her words felt like an anchor in a thundering ocean. I was grateful.

With that, I nodded, a slight and jerky motion, before turning back to the transmitter. The holo's faint glow painted my hands in a sickly hue as I grabbed it. I found myself hesitating, unsure where to start.

The transmitter's interface stared back at me, a cluttered mess of half-compiled code and cryptic error logs. I scanned the tangled lines, searching for something, anything, that stood out. My hands moved on instinct, driven more so by desperation than confidence. A mistyped command, an unchecked script.

"Focus," I whispered to myself, my voice barely audible over the faint hum of the holo. What would Finnegan do? My fingers were clumsy as they moved, pulling apart the chaotic lines of code one by one. I traced pathways, trying to understand what each strand meant. Each tap against the glass felt like I was mistakenly fraying a tether as I tried desperately to remember what Finnegan had taught me.

My eyes landed on a piece of broken code. I stared at it for a minute. The long chain of symbols and abbreviations was lost to me but split at the end. There was a brief sputter of hope before I noticed several more. Panic began to flood me as I realized this is where Finnegan had left off.

The intricate woven details of the code weren't chaotic, they were stitched together in perfect harmony, blending seamlessly into one another. Until now. I studied it, confusion pooling at the base of my skull. The code was nearly complete, but that didn't mean I understood it. I'd barely taken a few computer science classes, and this was well out of that realm.

I let out a huff. I tried writing a bit of code, but the lines looked cumbersome and wrong compared to the previous ones. I began to delete it, unsure of what direction this weaving line of intricate numbers and symbols was moving in. Another line of code left my fingertips, but an error message popped up on the screen. The familiar feeling of frustration began to bubble back up in my throat as I deleted what I'd written once again.

"Need help?" Jones's voice broke through, steady and grounding. I shook my head, clicking my tongue in annoyance.

"I'll manage." I let out a tense breath. "Keep working on whatever is probably happening in our bodies right now." My hands trembled. I wasn't sure if it was due to fear or fading adrenaline, but I couldn't stop. Not with so much on the line.

It felt as if I were waging war in the trenches of syntax and circuitry. Each and every command I hurled at the transmitter was met with defiance as the stubborn beast spat back error codes like a volley of arrows. The lines of code I wove with my fingers felt clunky, like a mismatched, crude tapestry unraveling before me. Error messages bloomed across the screen like tiny explosions, each one a reminder of my inadequacy. The faint, yet relentless pulsing of the green blinking light seemed to sync with the pounding in my skull, a cruel rhythm that refused to relent.

The Beast Among Us

Revelation 13:1

Most of the day had passed, though it felt like an eternity. My fingers grew stiff, their movements sluggish as exhaustion crept in. My head still throbbed with the machine's ceaseless blinking, a maddening strobe of light and pain burrowing into my thoughts. The gravity of it pressed down on me. The futility, the despair, the silence. I wanted to vomit.

Tears began to prick at the back of my eyes. I wanted to collapse under the weight of my frustration, the urge to give up and curl into a ball gnawed at me, whispering that this war wasn't mine to win. But still, I sat there, fingers trembling across the screen, fighting against the suffocating tide of defeat.

I took a moment, staring at the numbers and symbols. My attention flicked to the low oxygen warning in my helmet I had all but forgotten. The faint glow of orange was a nice change from the sickly blue of the holo.

I squeezed my eyes shut, trying to staunch the pain in my head as dread filled my bones. *What do I do?* My hands clenched around the holo, wanting nothing more than to feel it crack and splinter beneath my gloves, but I relented, choosing to take a few harrowing breaths instead.

I opened my eyes once more, the nauseating blue pooling in my vision like a hazy fog. I searched the contents of the code that Finnegan left behind. There had to be a pattern to them. I quickly scanned through the pages of code, scrambling to find anything familiar. I started to notice a few symbols that followed certain numbers, two lines that always seemed to end the function, and a new line that started after a specific symbol each time.

My fingers moved through Finnegan's notes. I scrawled through page after page of old codes, trying to find a pattern or pieces of what I would need in hopes of sewing it together with what was left. My confidence grew as I scrolled back to the transmitter's interface where the frayed edges of unfinished code remained.

Hope filled my chest as I started typing. The lines, though still a bit clunky, seemed to fit in with the original code better. As I flipped between the notes and interface, less error messages popped up along the screen as I moved. Sometimes the patterns didn't work, but a few taps at different symbols would move the lines along. As the error messages became less frequent, my fingers moved faster. Though it was a language I couldn't understand, it didn't mean I couldn't figure out the patterns, the syntax. As I worked, I felt a gnawing in my stomach. A feeling of dread and panic built low in my gut, but I continued.

Beep! I stopped at the loud sound against my ears. The transmitter no longer blinked. Instead, the green light remained steady. The screen of the holo flashed, and a dialogue box jumbled with woven symbols appeared. And, at the bottom, a blinking cursor underneath the word Message.

"Ha!" I jumped up, excitement filling me with renewed vigor. "I got it!"

I looked at Jones, and my blood ran cold.

She sat, slumped over her half-shattered console, unmoving.

"Jones?" My voice sounded feeble, but if she heard, she returned no response. My head began to ache from my sudden burst of energy, the lack of food and water hitting me. "You all right?"

There was a murmur, like a hushed and raspy word spoken but only for her to hear. I moved closer, worried but cautious.

"H-h." She didn't pick up her head as her body trembled. Her hands slid against the console, twitching as they fell to her sides.

"What?" I knelt next to her. My eyes widened. Her face was flushed as sweat poured down her features in thick rivulets, glistening under the dim light and pooling at the collar of her suit helmet. Her breathing was uneven, deep and erratic, as if trying to drink the air and failing. "Jones."

"Hot," she croaked, her voice tight with irritation. She suddenly lifted her head, her breaths turning to gasps as she struggled. Her movements were jerky and confused, as if she were being tugged along by invisible strings.

"Hey, maybe you should lie down." I moved toward her, but I remained vigilant.

Each motion she made was unsettling, like her body wasn't her own. Her hands flitted from side to side, grabbing at her suit and helmet, pulling them away from her body, but nothing brought relief.

"Jones?" I reached out a tentative hand, worry consuming me.

"God, it's hot." She slung an arm at me, missing my hand by a few inches. Her breathing grew more intense. She fell to her knees, taking deep gulping breaths. Her hands clawed at the helmet's edges, movements frantic and unco-ordinated. Her gloved fingers scrambled and slid over the smooth surface, searching for release. Each failed attempt only fueled her panic, her breathing ragged, creating bursts of fog that covered the inside of her visor.

"Jones, stop!" I grabbed her hands, trying to pull them away from her helmet. "Just relax for a second!"

She shook her head violently, tearing her hands from my grasp. The wheeze of labored breathing filled her hel-met, a suffocating rhythm that echoed through our speakers. Sweat continued to pour down her face, dripping into her eyes.

"Please," she begged in a raspy tone. Her voice itself seemed to be dehydrated. She tugged at the latches once more, but her hands slipped again, and a hollow *thunk* ech-oed through the ship as she slammed her hand against her visor.

I grabbed at her hands again.

We struggled, pleading with the other to relent, but Jones was stronger. Her hands tore from mine a second time before a click resounded as the helmet latch released. A hiss filled the air as she twisted her helmet, removing it from her suit.

I stood in shock.

Her body trembled as she hunched over, her chest rising and falling as she wheezed. Her twitching began to lessen as her breathing calmed, turning into slow, steady inhales, drinking in the air. Sweat dripped from her helmet as I picked it up, tearing the rebreather out.

"Here." I held out the rebreather in hopes she'd put it on, but she didn't move. Instead, she continued to sit and breathe, her broad shoulders turned inward. "Jones, you need to put this on. I can't lose you too." I knelt beside her.

Her eyes were alert, the pupils mere pinpricks in the deep golden brown of her iris.

In a flash, her hands were around my throat, her fingers digging in with crushing force. Her eyes darkened, stripped of mercy and reason. A snarl twisted her lips as a thread of saliva slipped from the corner of her mouth, mixing with the sweat on the floor.

Raw panic surged through my chest and arms, an electric form of terror that made me dizzy. My hands flew to hers, slapping and clawing desperately for leverage. I scrambled against her iron grip, the gloves covering my hands making it impossible to find purchase. My feet shuffled against the floor, trying to push me away, to escape, but she followed, pressing down harder, her weight sinking into me.

The world constricted, sound muffled beneath the pounding in my skull. A wretched wheeze escaped me, pathetic and small, swallowed by the violent shudder of my body as it fought against hers.

My vision began to blur at the edges, darkness creeping in at the corners. I thrashed harder, driven by mindless survival, but her grip would not falter. I realized I was no longer fighting Jones. She had become primal in every way. And I was losing.

"You will never take him away from me." She sneered, her forehead pressing against my helmet.

I felt the last of the air leave my lungs, and my movements slowed as I weakened. The world muddied around me, hazy and indecipherable. I was going to pass out soon. My hands fumbled around my suit, her fingers, but she refused to yield. I shoved against her with every ounce of strength I had left, my fingers stretching, clawing for her eyes. But they fell short, grasping at empty air. My chest burned, my vision pulsing to a small tunnel of light and shadow.

Then, without warning, her grip vanished.

I collapsed, my helmet hitting the ground first and hard, a ragged gasp tearing from my throat as air rushed back into my starved lungs. Each wheezing breath seared my chest like inhaling broken glass. I barely registered the feeling of the floor over the violent pounding of my heart and thundering pulse in my ears. My hands trembled against the ground, my muscles twitching as if rebooting and recalibrating.

I pushed myself up, a deep, racking cough scraping through my throat. My body heaved and my hands slipped, and I crashed to the ground once more. More coughs pierced my chest, and it felt like torture.

I tried pushing myself up, my vision still foggy. As I sat up, the world spun. Jones was nowhere in sight.

I let out a breath of relief and closed my eyes, trying to still the pounding headache between my ears.

Relief? My eyes snapped open. *Where did she go?* I scanned the room, gaze darting around frantically in fear and worry. I pushed myself up to my feet, my legs weak but steady.

"Jones?" My voice barely carried, just a rasping whisper torn from my raw throat. I winced as I stumbled my way out of the ship.

I could see the torn blades of the tall, unnatural purple grass where Jones had sheared her own path to the woods. Beyond the tree line, the darkness pulsed. Rhythmic flashes of violet and red tore through the trees, casting long, jagged shadows across the ground. The intervals between each burst were slowing, like a heartbeat losing strength.

Jones's course was written in those flickers, like a beacon calling out her every move.

I glanced toward the green light of the transmitter, torn.

The transmitter waited, steady and unfailing, its glow reflecting along my visor. Beckoning. I could send a signal. I could be saved.

I swallowed hard as I turned back to face the tree line. I had a choice to make. Follow Jones into the shadows and try to bring her back . . . or save myself. *Is she worth it?*

My breath hitched at my own thoughts. *She's my friend.* My legs refused to move, stuck. *Would she save you?* I scoffed. Of course she would. *Of course.*

My hands clenched at my sides as I watched the pulsing of the trees fade, each flicker growing weaker, slower. It felt as if, by letting her run, I could chase her from my mind and erase the weight that held my chest. But I knew better. I charged forward.

I crashed through the foliage, flashes of vibrant violets and reds ensuing behind me. Every flash made the trees feel more alive than they should be, shifting their limbs to close in. Every breath burned within my lungs as the tall grass whipped against my legs and hips. Ahead, Jones was barely a flicker between the cascade of shifting light, her form weaving through the twisted trunks.

"Jones!" I gasped, pushing forward. "Stop!"

The blades of grass clawed at my arms, gnarled roots jutting out from the ground like grasping hands threatening to send me sprawling. The terrain sloped unevenly, forcing me to fight for balance as I drove faster, desperate to close the gap between us.

The flickering of the lights was disorienting, warping the depth and distance at which she was ahead. The flashes of red and violet streaked across my visor, blinding me for moments at a time, distorting the world around me. Then they stopped.

I slowed, taking gulping breaths of air as I watched, waiting to see which direction the trees would signal next.

Before I could react, a weight slammed into me. The impact knocked the air from my lungs as the world spun violently. My back hit the damp earth, pain erupting through my spine as it crunched against my air tank. A sharp gasp tore from my throat as hands pinned me down.

"J-Jones." I coughed.

Her face hovered above mine, her breath ragged, her eyes wild.

The forest erupted in a brazen flash of light. For a moment, neither of us moved. Suddenly she raised a fist above her head before slamming it down against my visor with brutal force, the impact reverberating through my skull.

Terror chilled my blood as I flinched from another strike. A third blow followed as I scrambled to grab her arm.

It became an all-out struggle, both of us grappling for control. Limbs tangling as the grass ripped beneath us while we rolled through the dirt. The world blurred in dizzying streaks of violet and red, the flashing lights pulsing wildly, disorienting.

Jones fought like an animal. Every strike was fueled by something entirely unforgivable. I barely managed to free my leg and, with one meager kick, sent her sprawling back.

Panting, I pushed myself up, my body trembling with exhaustion.

"Enough!" I roared.

She stood opposite me, chest heaving, eyes burning, completely overshadowed by something dark and primal.

"We need to get back to the ship!" Spittle flew onto my visor, panic gripping me at the throat. My muscles coiled, waiting for her to pounce. The silence felt suffocating, the only noise our feet shuffling through the grass in a dizzying circle and my pulse loud in my ears.

"You will not take him from me again." Her voice dripped with malice as her gaze raked over my suit, searching for weakness.

"Take who?" My voice wavered, confusion tangling its claws with fear. In my moment of hesitation, my foot caught against a root, and I pitched slightly to the side.

She lunged. I barely registered the movement before her body tackled mine, sending us both crashing to the ground once more. The forest burned around us in shifting light, the trees glowing from within like fiery embers spreading through their veins.

"Jones!" I gasped, but she was lost.

Her fists rained down in an unholy tirade. I thrashed against her, squirming and struggling. She screamed as she released blow after blow, each strike harder than the last. Unbridled rage and pain contorted her face in an unrecognizable fashion.

I threw a single, desperate, clumsy punch, yet my knuckles managed to catch her chin. It was enough. She cried out as she reeled back.

I scrambled backward, crawling along the ground like a wounded animal, my lungs burning, my mind screaming.

Please stop. Please. I begged, but there was no mercy to be had. As I stumbled my way to my feet, I turned to look but froze.

Jones's body convulsed on the ground, limbs lurching in unnatural, jerking motions. A guttural noise fell from her throat as she twisted, arms flinging wildly.

Fuck.

Adrenaline screamed at me to run, to turn and bolt to the ship. *The ship.*

I searched frantically through the dense trees. *Which direction is it?* I spun in circles, head whipping. *Where?*

My eyes landed back on Jones. I could only watch as she staggered upright, blood trickling down her neck from the cut on her chin.

"This is insane." I pleaded with her, my voice barely more than a breath, begging with whatever shred of sanity she had left.

Jones took a step forward.

Instinctively, I stepped back. She tilted her head, a sick grin stretching across her face. "What're you going to do?"

"Jones."

"You going to kill me?" Her words dripped off her tongue like poison. "Like you did them?"

My blood ran cold, ice spreading through my chest. "Shut your mouth," I said, quiet but stern.

She laughed, the sound sharp and hollow, ringing through the dense audience of trees around us.

"I'm next, aren't I? Just can't help yourself, can you?" She sneered, spreading her arms wide in mock invitation as

I clenched my fists. "Did you act like a sniveling bitch when they fought too? Or did you sneak up on them while they slept? You seemed to have spared us the details all those years ago."

"Shut up," I growled. The grin on her face widened, eerie and twisted. "You have no idea what you're talking about," I spat, anger clawing its way up my throat.

"Don't I?" she taunted, her eyes gleaming. "At least when I lost my son, it wasn't by my own—"

I rushed her, not wanting to hear another word. Our bodies collided again, but this time it was my fists connecting. I didn't care where they landed. Blinded by savage wrath, pure and reckless, I couldn't stop.

She writhed beneath me, her hands failing to block my own, her legs desperately trying to find purchase to push against me, but I was merciless.

I sunk my weight down further, driving my knees into her ribs as my hands latched onto her throat. Blood poured from cuts along her face, her eyes wide with fear, but I refused to let go. Her nails clawed at my suit as I tightened my grip. Her eyes burned with fury, but she was growing weaker.

Crack! A sharp explosion of pain ricocheted through my skull as my vision jolted sideways, the impact ringing like a gunshot in my ears. My grip faltered, but before I could react, another blow landed, harder this time. A third strike.

Warning lights flared along my HUD. I let go. The rock struck again, skidding against my visor with a sharp screech, the final impact sending a web of fractures crawling along my vision. Each jagged line splintered the world around me, distorting the world into something broken and ugly. Air rushed into my helmet. I sat up, shocked. *No. No. No.*

The fragmented image of Jones convulsing on the ground met my eyes, the rock still clenched in her hand.

Blood smeared across her face, merging with the dirt in thick, uneven streaks that clung to her skin in dark clumps. I watched in both awe and horror as she screamed, flailing her arms and legs, tearing at the grass.

"Let me go!" she cried. "Get your filthy hands off me!" Her arms and legs twisted toward the air, the tree behind her burning in flashing vibrant reds and purples.

"Jones." My voice was barely a whisper as I reached a tentative hand out. My shattered visor made it nearly impossible to see clearly. My fingers toyed with the helmet latch, my heart racing. *No. This can't—*

Jones writhed on the ground, tears staining her face through the dirt and blood.

"I said let go!" She fought against invisible adversaries, yanking her arms back toward her body, her fingers fumbling against her pocket.

"Wait!" I dove toward her hand that was grabbing for the knife, trying to pull it away, but I was too late. She swung.

Piercing, sharp pain exploded through my right shoulder as I let out a scream. A sickening *squelch* echoed through the air as the knife slid free from my shoulder, sending a fresh wave of agony rippling through me. I moved away, clutching my arm to my chest, feeling the warmth of blood soaking my arm and suit.

"Get off me!" she screamed. As she flung the knife wildly, it connected with her own suit and skin, tearing cuts through each. "Get out!"

I watched in horror as she plunged the knife into her stomach.

"Jones!" My voice cracked as blood poured from the wound. She screamed as she tore the knife across her stomach in some ill-mannered operation.

"Get out!" she yelled through clenched teeth.

What the fuck. Thick, crimson blood flooded over the wound, her exposed entrails releasing the warmth from her body into the air.

The world spun, vomit settling in my throat. *This can't be real.* My hands clawed at the dirt, trying to grab hold of reality. *This isn't real.* My fingers tore through the roots of the grass, the leaves bending and falling over me as I shook. *This can't be real.*

The Valley of Dry Bones

Ezekiel 37:1-14

My stomach churned violently, the bitter taste of bile rising in my throat as the scene replayed in my mind like a cruel, looping nightmare. I fell back, the cold ground lurching beneath me, my hands grasping as the sky fell in a sickening tilt. My breaths came in shallow, ragged gasps, each one catching on the lump in my throat. The air felt too thin, too sharp, like my helmet was digging its claws into my chest and throat instead of allowing air to fill my lungs.

The image of Jones's knife tearing across her body burned into my vision. I squeezed my eyes shut, but the sight of her mangled flesh remained, more vivid, until it felt as though her death were imprinted onto my eyelids instead.

I scrambled back, my arms and legs flailing, my stomach knotting painfully. The forest seemed to shift around me, the contours of it twisting into grotesque, clawed shapes that loomed closer with every second. My vision blurred, sweat slicking my face.

I clutched at my helmet, fingers digging into the unyielding surface, desperate to silence the noise in my head. *It's not real.* It couldn't be. My own reflection in the visor stared back at me, hollow-eyed and pale. A stranger. Thoughts swarmed my mind, the noise growing louder, faster, like a storm building in power and force. *Wake up.*

"No," I croaked, barely audible, my trembling hands desperately grabbed at my knees as a cold, clammy wave rolled over my body. I gagged, swallowing hard against the bile rising in my throat. *I'm losing it.* "Stop, please."

My pleas were hoarse and unheard, my voice cracking under the pressure. I spoke only to myself, begging my mind to stop. The edges of my psyche had already begun to fray after Hoku and Finnegan, but now they unraveled.

I tried to think, to focus, but thoughts slipped through my fingers like sand. My heartbeat thundered in my ears, frantic and uneven. I couldn't tell if I was breathing too fast or not at all. The boundaries between me and the planet began to warp, my skin and suit becoming one, melding with the ground I sat on. *I'm fucking losing it.*

My mind was ablaze, shredding itself like a program being deleted. Logic was fading, reality tearing apart, and all that remained was the unbearable pressure. Every idea and every memory was ignited in a flash of searing light, consuming itself before I could grasp it.

I felt too full, too hot, like a reactor core melting down. The flames weren't physical, but they burned, a relentless inferno that licked at the edges of my consciousness. It threatened to engulf me. Utter chaos, raw, untamed, and unbearable, filled the space under my skin.

My skull throbbed, the sensation like molten metal coursing through my veins, radiating outward in pulsating waves. There was no escape. Sparks of pain ricocheted behind my eyes. Every attempt to focus just fed the flames. A scream caught in my throat.

I was being consumed. Burned alive from the inside out. My mind wasn't just on fire. It *was* the fire, a roaring blaze that would leave nothing but destruction in its wake.

My body felt foreign, like I was watching a movie of someone else trapped in endless horror. All the weight I carried finally came crashing down, splintering the very essence of my soul. I screamed again, the sound pushing the air out of my lungs with unimaginable force. The noise reverberated through the trees as I cried. *What am I doing here? How could this happen?*

I clawed at the latch for my helmet, ripping it open and tearing it from my suit. My fingers buried themselves in the cold dirt again, my tears mixing with snot on the ground as I screamed. A wild and visceral soul-ripping scream tore from my throat until there was nothing left. *Why?*

"Marcus?"

I froze. My rebreather stared at me from my helmet a few feet away. I knew that voice. *Impossible.* I didn't dare move.

"What's going on?" Her voice slid through my ears like a whisper woven into the very fibers of my being. My breath hitched. The forest was completely still, the silence deafening. *Impossible.* The smell of her perfume curled around me, unbelievably close, threading through my resolve. My pulse pounded in my ears.

"You're not real," I said, my voice barely audible.

"Honey." The word dripped into my mind. "You're hurt."

My fingers twitched deeper into the ground, the cold steadying me, but it did nothing to stop the whisper from sinking deeper into my bones. A sharp inhale. The forest held its breath. My mind screamed that she wasn't— *couldn't*—be here, but the air felt heavier, falling like a blanket on my skin. *I'm losing it.*

"You're not real." The resounding silence stretched just long enough for me to feel some relief. Then, right in front of me, breath warm against my skin.

"Are you sure?"

Panic filled my blood as I clambered back, my eyes flitting up.

My heart broke. For the first time in almost two decades, she stood before me. Her black hair glinted in the moonlight, an unearthly glow surrounding her silhouette. Her eyes were soft, a small smile on her lips.

I quivered.

She tilted her head in question, her long hair falling over her shoulder. She moved to check on me, her hands pushing my head this way and that, inspecting my shoulder, but I couldn't look away from her. Her eyes, her hair, her face . . .

Tears streamed down my cheeks, but I didn't bother to wipe them. I didn't want to lose a second of her.

"Dad?"

The air left my lungs at the small voice. I turned and there she stood, clutching that raggedy teddy bear I had won at the carnival for her first birthday. Her little pink dress was still perfect. *No, please.* She moved closer. *This isn't real.* I crawled toward her, my legs too unsteady to stand. I felt the warmth of her skin as I reached to touch her face, the softness of her hair. *Please.* I pulled her toward me, embracing her as sobs racked my body.

Please let this be real.

My embrace tightened in fear and my eyes squeezed shut. If I could hold on to her long enough, maybe I could stay in whatever timeline I managed to find myself in.

"Everything's going to be okay, Dad." Her voice was muffled against my suit.

I laughed at her words, tears pouring down my cheeks, and opened my eyes to look at their faces one more.

I was met with empty air.

No. No, no, no. I searched frantically, turning this way and that, hoping to catch a glimpse of them. "Bring them back!" I yelled into the night. "Please!" Cries shook my shoulders, my breathing shallow and hard. The pain of losing them for a second time felt unbearable. *Please.*

I closed and opened my eyes a few times, hoping they would return if I willed it hard enough. The forest remained silent, but then, a sliver of movement caught my eye.

A hand, small against the bark of the tree that lit up in violent colors, disappeared. I staggered to my feet, my entire body weak and trembling. I followed the burning pulse of lights from the forest once more.

With each step, it felt as if they were getting farther and farther away, the intervals between the lights growing. My feet moved faster and faster, pushing me toward a sprint. I gasped, each breath sharp and ragged, each step filled with agony. Sweat clung to my skin in a thick sheen, mixing with the heat of panic as I stumbled through the forest.

A muffled rumbling vibrated through the ground as I ran, my eyes searching for the source as I followed the lights. Then I saw it.

The trees were alive. Writhing limbs and roots stretched and clawed at one another like skeletal fingers weaving a prison around me. They moved with purpose, closing off my course just as quickly as they opened, twisting the world into an endless, pulsing maze of violet and crimson. My feet pounded against the earth, but no matter how fast I ran, I couldn't keep up.

"May!" My voice was smothered by the rumbling of the moving trees. "Wait!"

Their hands were everywhere and nowhere, slipping through the branches, curling at the edges of my peripheral vision. I knew it wasn't real. I knew they were gone. But I ran anyway.

The maze flickered, shadows folding into memories. I saw her. Her eyes, so achingly familiar, locked onto mine. I reached for her, but the moment my fingers were about to touch her skin, she vanished.

The forest twisted again, suddenly pushing me in a new direction, the earth changing around me, guiding me forward. A ragged sob tore from my body, but I forced myself to keep moving.

"I'm sorry," I choked, my feet tripping through the upturned dirt and roots. I faltered for a second, catching myself and shoving forward, chasing a past I knew I could never return to.

How could you? The words coiled around my ribs like a vise.

A figure shifted between the trees ahead. My heart slammed against my chest, desperate, pleading. The branches closed in, the maze shifting again. She was gone . . . and I was still running.

I didn't understand what could possibly be driving me forward. My body screamed in protest, my muscles were sore as exhaustion sunk deep into my bones, my stomach was void of food, and thirst parched every inch of me, yet I kept running. The maze shifted, the ground swaying as my vision blurred. My heartbeat thundered in my ears. The haunting smell of her perfume lingered faintly in the air.

And then I fell.

The world collapsed beneath me. I hit the ground, bones crunching and jagged rocks splitting my skin. I gasped as blood's metallic taste filled my mouth. Pain exploded through me as I came to a tumbling stop, but it barely registered. My blood froze. I couldn't process what I was seeing. The world stilled, my body aching, my mind struggling to make sense of it all.

Wreckage spanned as far as the eye could see, a sprawling graveyard of mangled ships, their twisted metal husks cracked open like rotting carcasses. Dozens, if not more, lay in ruins, each identical to ours. Their shattered frames bore the same name, *Revelations*, painted in our signature bold red. Sickly green transmitter signals blinked weakly from within the wrecks, flickering like dying stars scattered across a sky of ruin. The ground was thick with the remnants of the fallen. Skeletons lay sprawled in grotesque poses, their uniforms and suits—*my* uniform—torn and decayed, indistinguishable from one another except for the way they had been broken. Caved in helmets and splintered visors left hollow sockets staring out from within.

The ships were in various stages of decline. Jagged metal from the newer additions still gleamed under the alien sky, while others had long since surrendered to time, their husks buried beneath creeping vines and the thick, unnatural grass dusted in rust.

The planet had begun to reclaim them, tendrils of vegetation weaving through the shattered metal and glass. White, powdery spores floated lazily through the air, glinting in the light before settling upon the remains. The entire place was covered in it like a thick blanket. What was once machinery, purpose, and life, had become nothing more than remnants of the past.

Let There Be Light

Genesis 1:3

My eyes scanned the wreckage before me, my lungs devoid of air as terror coiled its slimy arms around me, digging into my skin and settling in my bones. As I stared at the massive burial ground, I almost felt at ease for a split second. The lights from the transmitters blinked in and out, reminding me of the small fairy lights that we'd string up during the holidays.

Exhaustion crept over me, weighing down my eyelids and filling my body with lead. I didn't want to move. Instead, I wanted to lie there in the tall, unnervingly purple grass and glowing trees, and pretend that I was back on Earth lying in a park.

It had been so long since I'd set foot on my home planet. If I closed my eyes, the dirt almost felt the way I remembered it. The way it formed to the contours of my weight, the feeling of the roots spreading away from my fingers as they dug into the soft, moist dirt. The air felt both cold and thick, sticking my hair to my forehead.

A light flickered to my left but not the same nauseating green as the transmitters. No, this was a white light, like those that lined the inside of a ship. I watched, waiting for it to happen again, thinking maybe I was just hallucinating again.

But there it was. A faint, wavering flicker from the shattered white lights within the nearest ship to my left, like a dying breath in the darkness.

I grit my teeth, forcing myself up, wincing at the sharp pain that bloomed along my shoulder and radiated through my bones. Once upright, I hobbled toward the lights. My movements were slow and deliberate, careful not to disturb the crumbling, lifeless forms strewn across the ground.

As I stepped inside the wreckage, a shiver crawled up my spine, making the hair on the back of my neck stand. The air was thick with the scent of rust and decay, and the silence felt cold and stark. Jagged metal gashes lined the hull, likely torn away during its violent descent through the trees.

A heavy knot of dread weighed down my stomach. Despite the ruin, the ship was unmistakably the same as ours. Perhaps an older model, but eerily familiar, nonetheless. The bridge was a mirror image of our own, down to the placement of the consoles and curvature of the walls. But here, nature had begun to reclaim its prize as blades of grass contorted their way through the cracked circuit boards and thick vines tangled among exposed wires.

A dusty photo lay against the captain's console. A family. As I picked it up, the dust fell from it, swirling through the air in lazy circles.

The mother and father held a small child, probably no more than a year old. Their smiles were wide and their eyes full of life. I placed the photo back on the console where it belonged, but my eyes remained glued to it.

"What do we do, Captain?"

My head jerked up, the words sending an icy spike through my spine, and my breath caught. They stood before me. Hoku. Fin. Jones.

Perfectly poised at their consoles, their backs straight, hands hovering over darkened controls as if awaiting my command. Their hands and bodies were covered in patches of white spore stalks pushing out of their suits and skin like fur spikes. The broken hull gaped in front of them, revealing the lifeless wasteland beyond, but they stood as if nothing had happened. As if they never died.

"What?"

Their heads snapped to me in creepy unison, their vacant eyes boring into me. I reeled back, nearly tripping over myself.

"What should we do next?" Their voices were layered in an unnatural chorus reverberating off the dead metal in a sickening mockery of unity. The sound crawled under my skin, digging deep, unraveling me from the inside out.

My hands clawed at my face, rubbing hard against my eyes. *This isn't real.*

"I-I." My throat closed, the words choked under the weight of bile and grief. *They're dead.* I had watched them die. I had seen their blood on my hands, witnessed their last breaths, and been haunted every moment since. "You're not real. You're dead," I croaked.

My mind spun, my pulse thundering in my ears like a deafening drum. Darkness crept along the edges of my vision.

Still, they watched, waiting. Small, unnerving smiles pressed against their lips.

"What are our orders, Captain?" The smile on Jones's face faltered, resetting too wide, too wrong. The others remained.

It's not them.

The air around me felt thick and suffocating, as if pressing in on all sides. The ship groaned, the walls seeming to breathe. I staggered back farther, my heel catching on something, dropping me to the ground. A skull, cracked and half buried in debris and dust.

"Stop," I begged.

"What do you want us to do, Captain?" They took a step forward.

"Stop." Panic clawed through my bones, freezing me in place. I watched in helpless horror as Finnegan's limbs snapped and contorted, his head wrenching to an impossible angle. Balanced on all fours, he began to crawl toward me as blood and spit fell from his mouth.

Above, Hoku clung to the ceiling, their neck splayed open, blood cascading to the ground as they mirrored Finnegan's grotesque movements. Every motion was jerky and cumbersome.

Jones hit the ground with a sickening, wet squelch. Her stomach split open, intestines spilling out along the floor, but she was undeterred, shoving them aside as she dragged herself forward with blood-slick hands. Black sludge oozed from their mouths and eyes, falling in thick chunks to the ground, yet their smiles never budged.

"Stay back!" I scrambled away, tears running from my eyes. *This has to be a sick joke.*

"What do you want us to do, Captain?" Their voices were gargled and gross as their procession continued. Their shadows drew long and ugly shapes along the ship's metal panels.

"Stop it!" My hands grabbed at my hair, squeezing my eyes shut, and willing them to stop.

I felt their hands clamber over me, pulling at my suit and hair, slipping against my skin as their blood covered me once again. A scream ripped from my throat. I could feel their rancid breath against my nose.

"What do—"

"I'm not your captain!" My voice echoed through the room.

"You—"

"I never wanted the responsibility." Sobs racked my body as they pulled harder, tugging at anything they could grab as I sat in the fetal position.

"Want—"

"I was never a captain." I pushed my head between my knees, the words falling from my mouth like vomit.

"No, but you were a father." My eyes tore open at the voice, *her* voice, but I was greeted with an empty, silent room. The edges of my thoughts began to unravel once more, like the loose ends of a severed wire.

Time felt as slow as the world around me was unpredictable. Reality and illusion were blending into a disjointed and surreal nightmare. I wiped the snot and tears from my face, taking a few shuddering breaths.

The ship, the planet, the weight of my own body. None of it felt solid anymore. Everything flickered and shifted between states of existence, like a corrupted hologram. My fingers tingled as I reached out, but for what? *Am I dead? Is this hell?*

The pressure in my skull built like a reactor on the verge of a meltdown. My mind caved in on itself, fighting to hold on, but the harder I clung to reality, the more it slipped from between my ears.

I looked back at the skull by my foot. It was still attached to the rest of the body, the person's holo resting in the crook of their arm. I reached down, pulling it free, careful not to touch the remains.

The holo was old but still intact, save for a few scratches along the front and a chip in the corner. A long wire had been messily spliced into the base of the holo, jutting out at an odd angle. I hesitated before tapping the screen, half expecting it to remain blank.

Instead, a dim glow sputtered to life. The holo's light was faint, casting a ghostly hue across my fingers. The screen sluggishly responded with a loading bar crawling forward.

When it finished loading, entry logs popped up. At first, each page was just the daily logs each of us was required to fill out. The daily chores and tasks completed, the samples and missions, new science or advancements, and all communications outside the ship. As I scrolled, the logs became more vague and less coherent. Then they stopped.

I flipped through several blank pages, ready to set the old piece of junk back against the corpse when a page popped up. A single word was written in the center.

Help.

I stared at it for a while, the blood draining from my face. My fingers hovered over the display before I forced myself to scroll forward. The next three pages detailed a story that felt impossibly familiar.

The story started with the crash of their ship, the crew's cautious exploration, the first unsettling discoveries about the trees, and their desperate struggle to survive. Supplies dwindled, hunger driving them to venture deeper into the woods to find food.

Then the madness began. It started with one crewmate unraveling at the seams, paranoia sinking its teeth into their mind. Within two weeks, four of their six members had succumbed, consumed by hallucinations and violent outbursts, tearing at each other for reasons unknown. The remaining two, battered and bruised, had made it to the graveyard. Desperately rifling through the other ships for any supplies, but none were to be found. What they lacked in supplies they managed to find in records.

Records? I scrunched my nose in confusion.

The next page was blank. A cold weight settled along my stomach. My fingers tightened around the holo as my pulse pounded against my skull. *Come on.* I scrolled through the pages, but they remained empty. I let out a breath of frustration. Closing out of the logs, I was about to toss the holo to the ground when I stopped. A small video waited at the edge of the screen. The play button stared back. I pressed it.

The video seized the whole screen, and a woman with short brown hair and green eyes sat at a console. Tears streaked down her dirt-covered face. She looked tired, her suit barely holding on to her thin frame. Her eyes were sunken and cheek bones pronounced. I recognized her from the photo on the console.

"I don't know how much time I have left." Her voice was soft, almost a whisper, yet urgent. "It's everywhere. It's in the air, the ground, the water, *everything*. I don't exactly know what *it* is, but whatever it is takes control of your mind. Once it's in, there's no getting it out. Once it has control, it's over." Sobs shook her body and shoulders as she echoed Jones's fateful words. "Please, you have to understand. They *lied*. They lied to all of us!" Her eyes left the screen for a quick moment, terror setting her pupils to pinpricks. "It's not real. Whatever you're seeing is not real. I don't know if there's a limit to how long one can stave off the hallucinations, but Amir lived for four days with the madness." She took a deep breath, and my heart slammed against my chest.

"I found the records. Apparently, most of us think alike." A small smile tugged at her lips as an uneasy laugh escaped her. Her eyes flitted nervously to the side. "Pretty much every ship out here had been collecting records for Revanche and investigating them, but none of us saw this.

This planet isn't *just* a planet. It's a living being. An entire, sentient, fucked up creature all its own. Somehow, someway, Revanche made a deal. To clear out their prisons on Earth, they decided to feed us to the planet, like some sick pet they keep at the edge of our zones." More cries fell from her as she put her head in her hands.

My eyes trailed back toward the outside of the ship and the planet's green moon floating lazily through the sky. It stayed eerily still, silent and unassuming.

My breath hitched, my chest seized, and my hands began to tremble. The familiar green rocky surface I had seen from space was gone. In its place, staring back at me in contentment, was an eye.

Vast and unblinking, it watched me with an uncanny gleam. Terror clawed through my throat, choking the scream before it could escape. My body was frozen in place, cold dread spilling down my spine. The entire time . . . It's been watching us the entire time.

"How could you?" May's voice rang through my ears in a shrill scream, and I tore my eyes away from the moon. She stood in the center of the bridge, wailing over the body of our daughter.

My heart wrenched.

"Why would you do this?" She pointed a crooked finger at me, her eyes dark, her teeth sharper.

I scrambled to my feet, my legs unsteady. "May." My voice wavered. I took a step forward. Tears stung my eyes.

"Our daughter!" she cried. Sobs racked her body as she fell to her knees, cradling the lifeless little body in her arms.

Blood stained her clothes and skin. I looked down to see a familiar, bloodied knife in my hand. My stomach dropped.

"No . . . I—" I tried to find the words, but my mind was a mess. *How?* My hands trembled.

"Why?" May howled. "How could you do this to her? My baby."

My mouth opened and closed like a fish, guilt and confusion swarming in on me from all sides. It felt like the weight of the world sat on my shoulders.

"Everything that has happened is because of you." Her eyes pierced through me, a hatred in them I'd never seen before. I stepped closer, my breath hitched. My daughter. My beautiful girl.

"How could you be so *weak*?" Her voice was sharper as it dug into my ears.

"What?"

"Is it too much for you?" She tilted her head. "The responsibility?"

"What?" My voice was small.

"Is that why you killed us"—she sneered—"and threw us out like trash?"

"I don't—" The bodies of my crew suddenly littered the ground, the knife growing heavy in my hand and dripping blood. It soaked the ground, traveling to me and up the fibers of my suit.

Panic clawed its way into me, my mind unraveling. I tried to wipe the blood away, but it smeared and congealed in an ugly mess on my hands.

"You couldn't even handle a ten-year-old, and they expected you to handle three adults?" She furrowed her brow. "How does it feel?"

My eyes snapped to the body of my daughter, anger bubbling within me as May stood.

"Stop it." I took a step forward, threatening. *It's not my fault.*

"How does it feel?" She drew closer. "To have the blood of the innocent on your hands?"

My voice wavered. "Enough."

"You're disgusting." Spittle fell from her lips as she spoke. "A vile, worthless, pig among men."

"*Enough.*" Anger swelled within me.

"Spineless." She shook her head, an ugly laugh escaping her. "A coward."

My voice was barely audible. "Stop."

"Did you like the way it felt?" She smiled.

"No!" The tears began to fall, the knife in my hand trying to pull me to the floor.

"You must've." Her face turned stoic. "Stabbing someone seventy-two times takes an awful long—"

"Shut up."

"You never loved us." She shook her head.

"I did!" I screamed.

"How could a father full of love tear apart his family?" she screamed back.

"You don't understand!"

"Of course, I don't, because I'm dead!" She flung her arms out wide. "And her, and her, and him, and them!" She pointed at each of the bodies on the floor.

I sobbed. "It wasn't my fault."

She crossed her arms. "Oh, but it was. Because you're a failure. An idiot they let aboard a ship with a crew who looked to you for all the answers. Little did they know . . ."

"That's not true." I shook my head.

She stepped closer, now only a foot away. "Yes. You'd think they would've noticed over the years how everyone pulled their weight on the ship but you."

"It's not true."

Her eyes moved along the bodies as she spoke. "Jones did all the driving and comforting. Most of the research was delegated to her and Finnegan. Poor Fin. He was just a kid and yet he still had more intelligence than you. Hoku did all the heavy lifting and they didn't even speak." Here eyes flitted up to mine. "What exactly did you bring to the table?"

"Shut up."

"Nothing."

"Enough!"

"Except you did do one thing right." She paused. "You brought them here and dug their graves yourself."

I felt the anger rising inside of me once more. "No."

"It's your fault," she spat.

"No." My hands and knees trembled, my breathing shallow, my vision growing dark around the edges.

"It was your decision!"

"Shut up!"

"You killed them!"

"I—"

"Admit it!"

"No—"

"You *wanted* them dead!"

I charged at her, plunging the knife into her body with a primal scream. Warm blood poured over my hands and pooled around the knife. I watched the life drain from her eyes for the second time, but instead of the familiar light of terror, a smile wound its way around her lips.

I stumbled back as she put a blood-soaked finger to her lips and ran her tongue across it.

"For what it's worth, you were quite the meal." She licked her lips as my vision turned and twisted, pain erupting in my chest.

I coughed, blood falling from my mouth in thick globs. I tried to breathe, grimacing at the pain. I grabbed desperately at my chest, my fingers meeting with a shard of metal, pain searing through me. My body ran cold. *How . . .*

". . . a normal life. They promised us freedom in return for dangerous work." The holo had continued the video, the screen just barely out of view as I tried to claw at the edge of the machine. "They knew we would die. They *knew.*" The woman's voice trailed off as she slammed her hand against the console.

"If you can hear me, it's already too late." She let out a tired sigh as the screen flickered. "You were dead the minute they let you out of your cage."

Acknowledgements

I would like to acknowledge my editor Anna for the extraordinary work she did to transform my muddled and repetitive words into something legible and truly finished. I would not be where I am without that help forward.

I would also like to thank the person who pushed me to get this book published. The person, who above all else, stood by my side every tireless hour of writing and brainstorming and countless minutes of me spoiling the plot. For that I am forever in his debt, for I would have never chased my dream if he didn't help me catch it first.

And lastly, to Skipper and Mags, for all the breaks in between and the hair stuffed in between the keys of my laptop, I love you both.

About the Author

A writer by night and an engineer by day. Kaitlyn studied and graduated with her bachelor's degree in chemical engineering. Following a long day of work she comes home to the little pitter-patter of paws upon the floor.

After dreaming incessantly of becoming an author, she finally took the leap. Each work of her works is nothing short of her heart poured onto the pages.